HOT

WET

TRAINWRECK

Copyright © 2020 by Mya Oh

HOT
WET
TRAINWRECK

a novel

for C.

CHAPTER 1
The Dick Cake Guy

Cue: *Darude – Sandstorm.*

Wait. *99 Luftballons*. That's a much better intro song.

No. That's not how I want to start this shit show. Or is this supposed to be a romantic comedy? You know, happy ending, lots of tissues, laugh-out-loud dialogue. Brilliant and sweet, with well fleshed-out, dynamic characters. Because that's usually a thing, isn't it?

And I'm already *rambling*.

So how on Earth do I start this? I'm twenty-four. Name's Bailey Finch. Yeah, that's a good name – it's not just my actual name, but it also looks damn good in print. A good, solid protagonist name.

And the guy? There's always a guy. I know you're waiting for *the guy.*

Well, what to say: Tall? Check. Muscles? Sorta-check. Tattoos? Check. Wry grin and one of those devious smiles akin to Ian Somerhalder? Check and check. One-thousand checks.

His name is Elijah Mattox. He's twenty-nine-years old. Favorite things that I've scrounged up so far include Asian-fusion cuisine, Single Malt Scotch, and perfecting his purposely-tousled hairstyle. He's an actor, trying to break into main-stream, silver screen. Accolades and Oscars.

As for now, well – he's only the most renowned Porn

Star in the country. Over three-thousand scenes to-date. Yeah, no kidding.

And here I am, sitting at my desk, pen in-hand, trying to conjure up some questions to ask him that don't consist of how many tits he's seen and what his thoughts are on the real-to-saline ratio. How many times could he climax in one session? Was his relationship with sex boring now? What is sex like once you've made a career out of using your cock?

Was he worried that working in porn might affect his career as a mainstream actor? This isn't some one-time Kardashian sex tape. Even though I'm sure he's got one of those floating around somewhere. The guy has history.

Then again, I've never actually seen his stuff. Never been much into porn. Even the soft-core variety. I mean, I've done a few Google searches in my time. I technically know what a penis looks like. One time in fourth grade, me and my old best friend, Ginny Weirkowitz, looked up *Two Girls One Cup*, and refused to eat for the rest of the day. Whatever you do, don't do it. Don't Google it. My eyes went to hell.

But IRL, I've never seen the real thing. I'm a virgin. And I don't say that to sound interesting, either: I've wanted to get laid more times than I could count. I have a vibrator, thank you very much. Have you ever used a Hitachi Magic Wand? Let me tell you...

I've just, you know, never had a real dick. I've never made love, had intercourse, fucked. Real hands, rough, desperate, passionate. Body-crushing. Mouth-on-mouth action. My only real kiss was Sophomore year of high school, on a dare, and that same guy ended up pouring an open container of spaghetti into my backpack after I reminded our Geometry teacher that he had forgotten to collect our homework.

I tapped my pen against the edge of my desk, glancing around the office: large windows, exposed brick walls, and blown-up copies of magazine covers from over the years, largely featuring notable men and women of the celebrity variety.

This was *Come's* first porn star. Clever magazine name, I know. *Come* as in: welcome, enter. *Come* as in...*orgasm.*

We were known for our sex tips and relationship advice. That said, it's been agreed upon that fucking in the shower just doesn't really work. I've never fucked a guy before, and even I can tell you that I know for a fact, unless maybe you've got one of those shower-bath combos or a seat in your shower, it's freaking impossible. I'd like to put out a request: if you're a woman who has had mind-blowing shower-sex while standing up, please write to me.

I grinned unabashedly, outwardly, probably looking ridiculous. I hadn't accomplished a lick of work in the past two hours. I couldn't concentrate. I was hungry: one of those gripping, all-consuming, carb-salt-sugar craving hungers. I wanted a pretzel, doughnut, and Diet Coke, stat.

What do you ask a porn, star, though? What are the questions?

I don't know, Bailey. Maybe treat him like a normal human male. Like a person. Like you.

I flushed at the thought. Like me, a virgin. A big-mouthed mope of a virgin, with brown hair that was frizzy on good days and unhinged on bad days. Shoulder-length. I wore loafers and slacks to work, button-downs with quirky designs. Today was yellow ducks. But Bailey Finch, as a whole, was painfully *un*quirky. I was a poser. Inauthentic. Maybe a little too self-deprecating. I was most authentic at home, in bed with my laptop, wearing a hooded sweatshirt, leggings, and cabin socks. The fluffier the socks, the better.

I wondered briefly what Elijah would think of me in comparison to the girls he'd been with on-screen. Did that even matter? No, of course not.

Still, I wondered. Maybe I should flat-iron my hair, or wear shoes with wedges. Lip-gloss vs. lip balm.

Procrastination: I typed out on the keyboard. *Failure to concentrate. Here are some random facts: Scotland has 421 words for 'snow'. Elephants are the only mammals that can't jump. The first oranges weren't actually orange. The most common name is Mohammed. Cats can hear ultrasound. Children grow faster in the springtime. Karaoke means 'empty orchestra' in Japanese.*

Delete. Roll eyes. Sigh heavily.

As I sat there, staring at a blank Word document, my boss, Deborah – a tall, all-limbs woman, popped her head into my cubicle.

"How are the interview questions going?"

Her expression was vaguely fatigued despite remaining without a single crease or line; her face was elongated, elegant. She had the most delicate bird-face. Long, a pointed nose, elven cheek-bones. Her eyes, two silver buttons, were wide, perpetually surprised. Her foundation was light enough that I could still see the subtle, natural gloss of oil on her forehead. She was, all said, pretty in a pained sort of way. Her ash-blond hair was always styled as if she were ready to step out onto a runway. She wore Louis Vuitton stilettos and a tailored houndstooth-print suit.

"Excellent," I lied. "I'm wrapping them up now, actually. I'll email them to you in a minute."

I'll email them to you in a minute. Panic. My heart jumped. Why did I always do this? I was a people-pleaser to my core, and it always, *always* ended up biting me in the ass. I lived in constant pause-or-panic.

"Awesome," she said, pleased. Her smile showed a bit of rose-pink lipstick on her front tooth. "Don't feel the need to get too detailed with them. Let him lead the interview, if you can. He seems talkative enough in past interviews. He did a very informative interview with *Cosmopolitan* last fall – we want to go deeper than that. Deeper than male skincare, workout regimens and how to maintain an erection, at least."

"Do you want me to confirm how many inches he is, exactly?" I inquired.

Deborah laughed.

"These are the imperative questions," she said.

"Yeah. If you can get his favorite lay, too, there's a good

one. Best orgasm story."

"I doubt his best orgasm has been on-film," I quipped. "I mean, three-thousand scenes. I'd be surprised if he wasn't constantly sore. I wonder if dick-fatigue is a thing."

"Then in a relationship! I don't really care. I just want the details and we can Jane Doe or John Smith the rest."

"Gotcha," I nodded. "I'll keep it professional. I'll keep it sexy."

While, of course, still focusing on the fact that he was now looking to step away from the Adult Industry. Maybe he wouldn't want to talk about anything sexual. He possibly wouldn't. Maybe he'd find it offensive – like a stain on his shirt that he was hoping nobody would notice, or an unruly cowlick.

Deborah scurried off in the direction of her next to-do, and I shook my head, a common mind-reset practice of mine. Like one of those Etch-A-Sketches.

Elijah Mattox, who are you, sir?

My fingers lingered on the keyboard, hesitant. I pressed my lips together, gave another heavy sigh, and then began typing. Twenty-minutes later, I had produced something palatable. Questions sure to please Deborah, while keeping it sexy, keeping it professional, keeping it to-the-point: Elijah, the whole person. Not just the lead in *I Didn't Know She Was Your Mom: Anal Edition.*

I sent the email off. As soon as I hit send, my pocket vibrated. It was also a known fact about myself that I wore pants loose enough to permit for large pockets. I hated purses. I had one, of course, but it contained mostly my wallet, a few old receipts, loose change and three Chap Sticks. I hated fishing for my phone, or taking the time to search for anything, really. Pockets simplify. It's a beautiful thing.

The text was from Charlie, my roommate.

Charlie: *Important. Come to the shop immediately. Consider this urgent.*

The shop, as it were, was the bakery Charlie worked at. It was infamous for its cupcakes and house-brew. It also offered a wide array of customized-confectionary.

I clicked my tongue, typing out a response.

Me: A*t work. Will stop by after.*

Charlie's reply was instant.

Charlie: *THERE'S A DICK CAKE HERE. YOU NEED TO SEE THIS.*

Charlie: *BAILEY.*

Charlie: *I KNOW YOU AREN'T WORKING. YOU HAVE THE WORST WORK ETHIC OF ANYONE I KNOW. HOW DID YOU EVEN GET THAT JOB?*

Calendar Editor, and through an excellent referral at university. It was more of an administrative role, entry-level, truth be told. I worked on the weekly calendar of events for the publisher. This was, officially, my first stint doing an actual interview. My first written-piece, scored through the fact that I just so happened to be replacing the original *auteur*, who was on Maternity Leave. Everyone else was swamped. This was my one chance, and it had to be good.

My phone vibrated again.

Charlie: *THAT WAS MEAN. I LOVE YOU.*

I tossed the phone into my purse with a soft *thud*, forgetting my pocket sentiments. Somewhere out there – that somewhere actually being a bakery in East LA – a Dick Cake existed, which apparently was a must-see. Akin to the Seven Wonders of the World. The Pyramids, or Stonehenge. A Dick Cake. Enough said.

The bakery smelled like burnt blueberry scones and buttercream. Baristas were pouring coffee from French Presses, their hair in updos – even the guys. Long hair was a thing here. They served pastries on small ceramic plates depicting clever quotes and tiny paintings of animals or *flora*, and espresso, tea, coffee from plain paper cups. No lids. Names were scribbled on the side hastily in black ink. One time I was Bali. Another time I was Bobby. I've been Bailie, Baley, and SO CLOSE – Baile.

Charlie was at the counter, grinning ear-to-ear.

"You best not be wasting my time," I told him. "I've got an interview to prep for."

"Oh, since when do you prepare for anything?" his tone was joking. He was an asshole, but a loving one. "I've got a date I should be grooming for, but I'm here, slaving away for the corporate giants."

"This place is a family-owned. There is literally no other *Pastries & Coffee* in Los Angeles, or anywhere for that matter. Also, great business name. To the point."

"Whatever. My pubes look like my dick has a bad

perm."

I shot a quick look over my shoulder to make sure he wasn't blabbering to listening-ears. Etiquette Police. The shop was quiet, with only a few sitting by the windows, lightly chatting, drinking their drinks and eating their croissants or danishes or tiny, adorable tea cakes.

"Who is it this time?" I asked. "Also, where is this aforementioned Dick Cake that you insisted I come here and see?"

He motioned for me to follow him behind the counter, into a small back-room. The counter was covered in frosting (I might have tasted it – vanilla marscapone) and cake scraps. A squat fridge sat in the corner, holding the awaiting custom orders.

I stole a cake scrap and popped it into my mouth. Ginger-lemon. Score.

Charlie carefully pulled the cake from the fridge, resting it on the counter. We both took a step back, just looking at it. Taking it all in.

There it was. Indeed a cake, shaped like a giant dick. Pubes and all.

"Well, shit, you weren't kidding," I muttered, candidly in awe. "Who is this for?"

Charlie shrugged. "Don't know. But the inside is almond and there's a chocolate-ganache filling. I wouldn't mind a slice of that D."

"You are the worst," I said. He slid the cake back into the fridge, and we walked back out to the storefront. "I'll take a coffee, black, and a Bear Claw. And tell me about this date."

"Their name is Sacha. Pronoun: *they*. Likes watercolor, wearing combat boots, and The Aquabats. Most importantly, DTF."

"DTF," I said. "What, are we still in high-school?"

"They *literally* said it," Charlie said defensively, whipping out his phone. There it was, a text from Sacha, reading: *whatever you want to do. I'm DTF.* "Besides, I'm not *expecting* anything. Just hopeful. Really hopeful. If not, we'll enjoy the extended version of *Lord of the Rings: Return of the King* celibately, and I'll enjoy my blue balls."

"Follow your bliss," I told him, taking my coffee and pastry. "Just be safe about it."

"And you watch out for tall men in sunglasses," he replied. "Behind you, Bailey. Oh God."

I turned, completely oblivious, and knocked straight into said Tall Man in Sunglasses.

The sharp sunlight cast shards through the window, and in the harsh brightness I couldn't really make out his face –but I knew he was grinning. Grinning and soaked in hot coffee. Hot coffee that I had spilled, all over him, because of course I did.

"Ohmygod," one word. I choked. "I'm so sorry! Do you want a napkin? No, a towel. I could get you a towel."

Charlie tossed a rag over the counter, and Tall Man grabbed it with an acknowledging nod.

"It's fine," he said, blotting the fabric. "Trust me. It's a shirt. I have others. Besides, this isn't the first time I've dealt with a spill."

"Oh."

Great reply, Bailey.

"Me either," I stuttered. "I spill stuff all the time. I'm pretty much a walking mess."

He laughed. I tried to find his eyes behind the sunglasses, but I couldn't.

"You're a little weird, aren't you?" he said, placing the rag on the counter. "Like one of those girls who wasn't very popular in high-school because they preferred wearing a Harry Potter house robe instead of normal clothes, and hung out in the teacher's lounge, and watched BBC at home with your cat."

"What the fuck kind of person says that to a complete stranger?" I snapped. "You don't know me, dude."

Tall Man laughed.

"You're right, dude," he said. "So tell me, what house are you?"

"Hufflepuff."

"Of course you are," he said, and then: "I'm a Slytherin."

"Bullshit."

"I have a Sorting Hat on my keychain. Here, look:" he pulled his keys out of his pocket, and there it was. It glinted in the sunlight. "See? Guys can watch BBC at home with their pets, too."

I studied him. Dark hair, obviously fit. Even though it was a wretchedly hot day outside, he wore a black T-shirt and gray hooded sweatshirt, so I couldn't quite see his body. I tried to fill in the spotty imagery with my imagination: sinewy, strong, not an ounce of fat. He didn't look like a guy that ate carbs. No bagels. No muffins. No Bear Claws, obviously. What a miserable life.

His smile was coy. His lips pulled at the corners teasingly. From over the counter, Charlie was on his phone, unphased. The shop had emptied; the afternoon lunch drizzle having dried up.

"Enjoy your afternoon," he said. There was a distinct conclusion to his tone. The conversation was over. A sense of tension hung in the air; I was intrigued at how someone, with a simple three words, could be so commanding and yet apparently had a nerdy streak.

How nerdy? I wondered briefly. Like, cosplay nerdy?

"You too," was all I could say. I didn't bother asking for another coffee. I could feel the paper bag wrinkle in my fist, still holding my pastry. My stomach grumbled. "See you around."

I wouldn't, of course. He was just a passerby. I decided it was best to leave.

From behind me, as my hand touched the door, I could hear his brief banter with Charlie: light, nonchalant. And then, as if by some stroke off magic, he said:

"Just here to pick up an order. I'm the Dick Cake Guy."

I smiled inwardly, pure satisfaction: like the first pop of a pretzel bite into your mouth. Buttery, delicious, so unhealthy but oh-so good.

See you never, Dick Cake Guy.

CHAPTER 2
Elijah Mattox: Fuck Machine & Part-Time Human

The address was scribbled on a Stick-It note, in faded ink, of all things. I squinted at the writing and plugged the address into my phone. *Ping.* Like Magic. And we were on our way – the royal we, so to speak.

As I drove, stuck in bumper-to-bumper traffic, I wondered what the house of a porn star would look like. Los Angeles real estate was outrageous, to be sure. But if this guy had been in over three-*thousand* films, I'm sure he's made a decent profit.

But who knows, maybe he was of the modest type: simple condo, maybe two stories. Overlooking the highway, even. A small backyard, avocado-colored stucco, a leaking sink and linoleum instead of ceramic or marble tiling. Maybe he didn't even have a yard. Maybe his house didn't even have windows. Do they make houses without any windows?

Okay, I'm getting ahead of things here.

He's not *just* a *porn star*, I reminded myself. He's a person.

But if I, an unknown to his work, couldn't shake the label – I couldn't imagine how the general populous viewed him. A big, hard, wet dick ready to fuck at a moment's request. A half-man, half-fuck-machine. A part-time human.

Elijah Mattox: Part-Time Human.

I fidgeted with the radio, searching for something. I didn't keep music on my phone, although I did enjoy podcasts. *Daily Fresh*, or *Mental Illness Happy Hour*. I was big on escapism. Maybe that's why I got into writing. Maybe that's how I ended up here, driving through the golden-tinted streets; the smog thick enough that I could almost feel it on my skin. I could feel a sense of tension, nervousness, trickling over me like a cold stream.

I looked around, feeling threatened by the grocery store signs and billboards advertising expensive lawyers and lip injections. All of the colors seemed muted, and the people walked – children and elderly alike – like the day was of no consequence. The boys buzzed by, like insects, on their longboards. The girls with long legs and puckered smiles posed on the corner, taking selfies. Everything was a shade of glitter and self-indulgence and a longing for beach waves. Salt water, cleansing. When was the last time I took a bath? When was the last time I had actually *relaxed*?

Good grief. And yet I still question why I've so fantastically failed to get laid into my near-mid-twenties.

I focused on the radio: Taylor's Swift's *The Man*. A great distraction. I sung along, chorus and all, in my crackling, pitchy glory. When the song ended, I pulled out my phone (at a red light) found it on YouTube, and played it again.

I kept it on repeat until I reached the destination: the abode belonging to Elijah Mattox. Which was, indeed, not a condo, apartment, or even the modest single-family ranch.

It was huge, plainly fucking huge. It had a gate, of all things – a golden gate – and a long, winding driveway, and Roman-style columns at the entrance. There was a single tower, complete with Romeo and Juliet patio. The structure itself was sprawled out; sort of gray-purple color, with what seemed like a thousand windows that promised the glimmer of something fascinating inside. They were like candles in the late-afternoon twilight.

This was some *Real Housewives of LA*-level shit.

The gate opened, as if on cue, and I pulled in hesitantly, sluggishly. I putted my way up to the grand entrance, parked, and paused. I sucked in a deep breath.

I'm a professional, I told myself. Who cares how big his house is? I could have a house this big if I wanted to, some day. It's just a house.

I grabbed my bag, got out of the car, and slammed the door. Another deep breath. Another reassuring mantra chanted under my breath. Each step I took towards the door made me feel dizzy, floaty. I didn't feel faint, but rather like I was stepping into something that I could in no way prepare for. Out of the comfort zone, out of the bubble. The virgin, the porn star. Hell, it could be a comedy.

At the door, I knocked. There was tense period of waiting; it hung heavily, like a gilded bell waiting to be rung. I waited for any sound. I didn't hear a dog bark, or footsteps, or anything at all.

Instead, he simply opened the door, like he was

waiting for me, and of course he was.

We looked at each other. In unison, we squinted. My mouth opened, slightly agape, like a codfish.

"It's you," I said. "You're the Dick Cake guy."

"Elijah," he preferred. His smile was soft, his eyes without the sunglasses a soft blue. Pale, but not cold. There was nothing electric in the way he stood, the way he looked. He looked warm. Welcoming. Like he could be somebody's husband, son, brother – father, even. "Or Eli. Eli is fine."

He looked like a regular person. Because of course he was.

"Well, I'm Bailey," I told him, half-laughing, wholly floored. "You can call me Bailey. I'm with *Come Magazine*. I'm here for the interview."

"I'm shocked," he smirked. "I had no idea this was an interview. I thought you were picking me up for a date. What's a girl to think now?"

He laughed at himself. But it was nice – sincere, light. He opened the door a bit more, and light from the hallway poured through from the many windows.

Stepping aside, he gave a commanding wave to follow him.

"Anyway," he said. "Let's do this thing. I've got places to go and people to see."

"Is that really true?"

"No," he confessed. "I've got a bag of Doritos that I haven't opened yet. Sweet Chili. And I'm back-logged on *Broad City*. That, Bailey, is my actual afternoon."

"Riveting."

Another smile, another nudge. And, because of course I did, I followed him inside – briefly forgetting why I was there in the first place.

Which that, I'll say, was a first.

I could feel my leg jump as I sat on the sectional, waiting for him, curiously glancing around. The entire place was open-air, and the windows gave it a light, almost ethereal feeling. There were plants everywhere – shades of green, blue, purple. Not the type of color scheme or décor theme I was admittedly expecting. Then again, what was I expecting? A heart-shaped bed in the center of his living room, complete with burgundy plush-top comforter and retro-colored throw pillows?

"I'm going to guess you prefer sweet to dry," Elijah echoed from the kitchen, mixing drinks. I watched as he zested an orange peel, running it around the rim. "I prefer dry myself. Maybe it's my sense of humor. Anyway, here's *Wonderwall*."

I observed quietly as he brought the drinks out, setting them down on the glass-top coffee table, seating himself next to me carefully. I felt, in that moment, both a stranger and like we were long-time friends.

I took a sip of the drink – citrusy, almost viscous. It lingered sweetly in my mouth like a slice of candied fruit.

"So," I started, shuffling papers. A lot of my work involved shuffling papers. Clearing throats. Double-checking that I had the correct dates or events and proof-reading for any last-minute errors or omissions. "First things, thank you for having me. We were pretty elated when you accepted our invitation for an interview."

"Big fans of my work?" he asked, and I couldn't tell if he was joking. His grin was slanted, playful, his eyes searching. "You, personally, a fan of my work?"

"I-" another throat clear. "I've never personally seen your work. You're just very well known. The *Ryan Reynolds of porn stars*, they say. Funny, charming, handsome."

"Ah," he sounded disappointed. "So you've never seen *The Domination of Elia Rose?* Or *Snuff Sluts*?"

There was a long, swollen pause. We simply watched each other for a moment.

"I hate the word," I said. "I won't repeat it."

"Me too," he agreed. "I mean, I hate the word. But to be clear, it's my most popular title. We did an all-anal edition last year, too. It was a massive hit. Paid for the cabanas by my pool and the sauna in my bathroom."

Anal. Fucking sluts. Snuff flicks. Was that legal? And here I was: barely kissed. Arguably frumpy woman-child. But moreover, *not* here to focus on his past filmography, but his future. I was here to talk about The Man: Elijah. The human side of him.

"Part-time human," I murmured to myself, and his eyebrows arched.

"Excuse me?" he asked.

"I just mean," I fumbled, embarrassed. "You're venturing into mainstream acting while still working in the Adult Industry. I read an article about it on Hexagon. Are you worried about the two conflicting?"

"No," he said plainly. "It's a different time."

I nodded.

"It also said that you've partnered with a new agent after having disagreements on the set of your last shoot. That seems to have stirred up some controversy."

His eyes quickly lowered, his shoulders hunched. We sat together on a sectional couch long enough to fit the entire revolving cast of *Grey's Anatomy*, but we were close enough that the silence of his breath was audible.

"My former agent and I had a good run," was all he said. "It was an amicable parting. I had artistic disagreements with him, that's all."

"What were the artistic disagreements?"

"You surely do not want to know."

Of course I did. I so, so badly wanted to know.

"This is all off the record," I reassured him. "This is just – I don't know – you and I talking."

He raised his eyes, quirking a smile.

"I didn't want to fuck the actress they paired me with. I could tell she didn't really want to be there. But she was there, technically agreeing. Technically willing. It was just – a vibe, really. I'm sure you've had those moments. Where you're sitting next to someone, and you just sense something. Well, I sensed that she was too young to really know what she was doing."

"Arguably the case for most young women that enter the Adult Industry."

"Fair enough," he concurred. "But she was eighteen,

looked twelve, and this was a hard-core scene. I'm talking choking to the point of tears, eating out of dog bowls, whipping."

"Fuck," I muttered. "Dog bowls?"

"Oh yeah," he continued. "Dog bowls. Fucking while their head is submerged under water. Asphyxiation. Scat play. Gagging. Humiliation," he listed the words off as if they were items on a grocery list, unphased. "Lots of tears. I couldn't do it, so I didn't, and they found someone else who would. Anyway, I'm much happier with my new agency."

He looked outward, beyond the windows, as if watching something hiding in the trees. Then, he turned to me again.

"Do you still do hard-core work?" I asked.

"Yes," he replied without pause. "It's what I'm most known for. I enjoy it."

"I guess I'm shocked that it's so staggeringly popular," I said, truly surprised. Sincerely naive. "How could someone get enjoyment from another's suffering?"

"It's not suffering if there's mutual consent and enjoyment," he replied. "Nothing is really boxed-up anymore. I'm surprised that you aren't aware of how deep desires can delve. We don't have limits anymore. Well, maybe one or two. But I guarantee you could still find them if you looked hard enough. We want what we want."

He sat back, watching my expression. He raked a hand through his hair – ash-brown, long, maybe a little shaggy. His lips pressed together, then parted. He was waiting for my reaction.

"I don't know if I'd want those things," I finally said. "But I can't say I really know what I want."

"Exploration," he said. "It's all about exploration. Self-exploration, exploration with a partner. But self-exploration is probably the biggest thing. Anyway, you're pretty, you're witty, you're obviously sharp. Partner or not, you'll eventually figure out what satiates you."

"*Satiate* feels a little dramatic," I said. "Perhaps satisfy."

But then again, was it, really? How far would I go to cum when I wanted it badly enough? I'd had enough close encounters with Charlie coming home early from work, vibrator buzzing, near climax.

And I didn't stop. I wouldn't have, even if he walked in. I wanted to cum badly enough.

"We'll see," I added. "And I'm arguably very plain-looking on the scale of objective attractiveness."

"You're like a young Jennifer Connolly, circa *Labyrinth*. You have a beautiful facial structure. Perfect eyebrows. You can't pencil in those brows."

"Well," I floundered. "I'll take your word for it."

He crossed his arms, quieting again. His eyes narrowed softly.

"You can ask me your other questions now, if you'd like," he said. He took a drink from his glass, the first time since having poured it. "Who I am. Eli. Or as you so quietly stated: Part-Time Human."

I slid my notebook and pen from my laptop bag. I

kept these things hand-written. I found it easier to articulate myself.

"I only mean, rather," I chose my words carefully. "How people outside of the Adult Industry, or those in the mainstream industry, view you. You said a minute ago that it's a different time now."

"Part-Time Fuck Machine, Part-Time Human, Full-Time Cynical Comedian," he sang. "I'm kidding. How do you think they view me?"

I was not prepared for that question.

"Like a regular person?"

"Is that what you really think?"

"I'm not sure what to think."

He smiled, took another drink. The glass left a condensation ring on the table-top. His eyes, as they shifted from my own, down to my chin, the curve of my neck – and then, *halt*. They felt like fingers. My throat tightened.

"Ask me the generic questions first," he offered, and I breathed. Deeply. A welcomed breath. "If it please you. This is a very disorganized interview."

That it was. I wrestled briefly, thinking of a reply.

"Happily," was all I said. "So you're twenty-nine."

"Thirty in September."

"How old were you when you entered the Industry?"

"Eighteen," he said, unmoving. "I grew up in a squat, beige-colored stucco ranch in Mulberry, Florida. We had gator living in our backyard for a time. I named him Snappy. He tried to eat me once, so Animal Control took him away. No money. Mom was a cashier at the local

Winn Dixie. That kind of thing. What you'd typically expect, I guess."

"So you did it out of necessity?"

"Yes," he said plainly. "And I'd say it worked out pretty well."

I looked at the questions I'd written out: there they were, and yet I was struggling to find the words.

"What was your first scene like?" I asked him. "I know that was eleven years ago. Do you still remember?"

"Of course," he said. "You don't forget your first."

"Would you care to share?"

He crossed a leg over the other, then glanced up at the ceiling fan. It spun lazily, as if in slow motion. There was no moving air to be felt.

"It was on the set of this big mansion in Tampa, FL. Not uncommon, mind you. We'd often use rooms and pool areas, you know, that sort of thing."

"I did not know," I informed him. "Continue."

"So," he continued. "I fucked three women that day, actually. It was a hostage scene. Very *Marquis de Sade*. I wore my first fitted suit that evening. The girls were naked, except for their underwear. And it wasn't sexy underwear, either. Plain white panties, their hair in braids. They had metal chokers around their necks, chained to the wall. Their wrists were bound with rough cloth. I fucked one while she drank water from a metal bowl, lapping it up like a cat. I fucked the other while a colleague watched, jerking himself until he came all over her face. The last, I fucked anally, against the wall, with her hands pinned. I pulled her hair. I came all over her back.”

“How did it end?” I asked.

“After I ejaculated,” he said, eyebrows arched, as if he'd already given the explanation. “And then we all cleaned up and went to Denny's for pancakes. But you know the craziest part?”

“What?”

“That was my first time. I was a virgin.”

Holy shit. What a way for someone to lose their V-Card. I couldn't do it. Not like that.

I could feel myself stumbling, internally. Eli chuckled, maybe at me, or maybe thinking back to that scene. He seemed to treat it like some sweet, fond memory.

I didn't know what to make of it – but I suppose that wasn't the point. It was acting, after all. How could I possibly understand, having never acted, having never even engaged in the act?

I sighed lightly, flipping through the papers even though the notebook lines below my written questions were blank. I needed a moment.

“Do you have any siblings?” I asked next, unintentionally soft.

“No, only child. I did have an eighteen-inch box television set, though.”

He was making jokes again. I couldn't read his expression. The soft, gentle, every-day man that I'd first caught a glimpse of when he opened the door had disappeared somewhere.

"What do you read in your spare time?" I asked. "Or watch, besides *Broad City*."

"Graphic novels, mostly," he said. "*Asterios Polyp*, anything by Adrian Tomine. There's a fantastic novel called *Here* that snapshots a single room, page by page, over the years. It's haunting. Television? I like *Shameless*, *The Crown*, *Downton Abbey*."

"So you like to laugh. And Period pieces."

"Of course," he said. "Everyone likes to laugh. Next question."

He grinned broadly, expectantly.

"What drives you?" I asked. "What drove you to become arguably one of the biggest adult stars of all time, and what drove you move away?"

He took a small breath, his eyebrows falling.

"Passion," he said plainly. "I was passionate about escaping my circumstances. When my Mom died, I was passionate about building a life that was better than what I'd been dealt. For awhile, it was passion in the literal sense: I love fucking. I love fucking beautiful women. I love getting paid to fuck beautiful women."

"Do they love getting fucked by you?"

"Yes," he said. "I dated a few, as well. Good chemistry makes for the best sexual sort of artistry. But that's just it: passion. And then one day, I had a disagreement. That disagreement led me to realize that while I still enjoy working in porn, there's other roles I'd like to pursue. Other experiences I'd like to have. I'm sure you can understand."

"What role do you see yourself in?" I asked,

scribbling quickly. "What's your ideal character?"

"What a question," Eli mused. "I'd say comedy. Dark comedy. Serial-killer meets stand-up comedian, or late-night show host. A notable figure, someone everyone knows, but doesn't really know at all."

"And that's something you can relate to?"

Our eyes met, as of course they would. A tender moment, albeit brief. He parted his lips, waiting before speaking, uncertain.

"Sure," was all he said. "Absolutely."

He picked up his glass, draining the remnants. I could see the orange zest floating at the bottom, the maraschino cherry having gone untouched.

"I suppose the last thing," I said. "They typically like a good picture for the articles. Something natural – a candid. You sitting on the couch is fine, even."

I rustled the camera from my satchel, not exactly the photog. But I could snap a clean photo, and for these purposes, that's all we needed.

Besides, he was a good-looking guy. This wouldn't be difficult.

I took a few steps back, focused, and shot. I took a quick peek at the preview: a sullen, steady expression. A slight tug at the corner of his mouth, suggesting a smile. Perfect. It would look superb in a black-and-white filter.

"Thank you," I said, ever the professional. "I appreciate it."

"My pleasure," he said, leaning forward. "Does this mean we can watch *Broad City* now?"

"Excuse me?" I shoved the camera back into the bag,

questioning my hearing for a moment. "You want me to watch television with you?"

"And eat Doritos, yes. I could order something if you're hungrier."

I stood, a little wobbly, but catching myself. Standing, I was well above him. I, the Giant, and he, the ant.

"We don't usually stick around after the interviews," I said. "It's very to-the-point."

"One episode," he said. "One episode, a single Dorito, and that's it. I swear."

He looked so hopeful, like a Golden Retriever waiting patiently for his owner to drop a milk bone.

"Fine," I conceded. "One episode. But I don't like Doritos. That stuff gets on my fingers and never washes off."

"Pretzels, then," he said. "I have the ones you can microwave, with the big chunks of salt. Or you could put butter and cinnamon on it."

Pretzels? Okay, so maybe this was fate. And here I was, talking snack-food with Elijah Mattox.

"I'll take one pretzel," I told him. "Hold the salt. Yes to the butter and cinnamon. Don't forget a napkin."

So that was it. I ate the pretzel, and we watched a single episode, and there was really nothing more to say about it. I heard his laugh a couple times – like a bell. He ate loudly, crinkling the bag as he dug his hand in, rummaging around as if searching for the perfect chip. Which exists, we all know this. The folded chips are the best ones.

"Enjoy your night," he said at the door. "Bailey Finch."

"You too, Eli," I said. "You know, you're a very strange person."

"Incurable," he said. "If you spend enough time with me, you'll find I'm not that alluring, either. But I make an excellent Greek omelet if you ever spend the night."

Wait, was that a suggestion? Did he expect for me to come back?

My heart jumped, much to my own chagrin. I could feel my face flush.

"There's a party I'm throwing tomorrow night," he said. "It'll be here. There's going to be cake, alcohol, other folks from the Industry. You're welcome to come if you'd like, if you want to keep talking about things."

"Things," I was amused. "There's more you'd like to include in the interview?"

"Possibly," he smirked. "It starts at seven. Wear a nice dress. Cocktail attire."

"Do you really think I own a nice cocktail dress?"

"Any dress, then," he shrugged. "I'm sure you'll look beautiful."

There was a sincere sweetness to the words. Like he really meant it. I couldn't help but smile. My heart was a skipping stone.

"I'll take your word for it," I told him. And then, I swiftly left before he could say anything else.

At home, safe in my room, I stared into the glow of my laptop screen in an otherwise dark room, thinking about Eli, the interview, the person. There was obviously so much more to him. I could capture it well enough in an interview, sure. It was compelling, smart, sharp, even, as he had called me. He was clever. It was sexy.

But that didn't *satiate* me, to use his verbiage. My fingers brushed the keys, my breath was low. I glanced at the interview questions laying sprawled on my comforter, the writing almost illegible in the darkness.

I began typing. It poured out of me. The entire experience.

The Dick Cake Guy, the serendipitous interview. The coincidence of Elijah Mattox being one and the same. The fucking, the dark, seedy inclinations of today's porn-viewing pool. Mulberry, Florida. The alligator in his backyard. The sad boy with the tiny box TV, watching episodes of Thunder Cats on a frayed living room rug while his mother slept on the couch. His mother, now dead. And he, an icon, relentless.

Full-Time Human.

When I stopped, it was morning. Saturday, thank God. The sun had barely crested, and Charlie hadn't yet come home. I poured myself a bowl of cereal, ate it precariously in the unlit kitchen, and slunked back to bed.

I contemplated the saved draft on my laptop, half-paranoid, half-proud. I didn't want this to just be an interview piece, but what if my boss didn't like my ideas? What then? The last thing I needed was to piss

Deborah off by going rogue.

As I sat, deep in the throw of a thousand different thoughts, my phone buzzed. A text. It was Elijah.

Elijah: *I really hope you come tonight. It would be super cool.*

I couldn't believe this was a thing: here I was, going to the party of a porn star. With other porn stars. Why? To see Elijah, I suppose. To get more dirt on him – but beyond that, to understand.

I liked him, in complete sincerity. He was hot, to be sure. But he was also funny, gritty and seemingly true.

I also really, *really* wanted a slice of that dick cake.

CHAPTER 3
Panic Party In the Hills

I slept until noon, when my phone, which had fallen to the floor, began bouncing from the vibrations. My ringtone – Beyonce's *All The Single Ladies* – was muffled against the rug.

I picked it up, hair stuck to my mouth, groaning inwardly.

"Hi, Mom."

"Bailey," she began. "I've called four times already today. What are you doing, sleeping til' noon?"

"You don't think four times is a little deranged?" I asked. "Is someone dead?"

"I could be!" she exclaimed. "But you'd have no idea, would you, sleeping until noon. I'm telling you, Bailey, you need to get out and start walking. Maybe take a spin class. Get yourself up nice and early. Do *something*."

"It's good to hear your voice too, Ma," I said. "What's going on?"

"Oh, baby," her voice softened. "Andrew, from synagogue, he died last night. Massive stroke. We're all devastated."

"So someone *is* dead," I said. "Wasn't he in his seventies? Didn't we go to his grandson's Bar Mitzvah?"

"Yes," she said. "Ezra. The handsome one with the dark hair. He liked you, you know. Absolutely smitten. We were all hoping something would happen between you two.”

“I'm very happy here in LA, Mom. I don't miss New Jersey. Well, maybe the deli sandwiches. But that's it. Anyway, I'm sorry to hear about Andrew. I'll send Ezra my condolences.”

“Well, I didn't just call to talk to you about Andrew, Bailey,” my mother teetered off. “I was cleaning out the attic and came across some old photo albums of your father's. God knows I don't want them, and with your father being God-knows-where with that damselfish-mouthed Leslie, I wanted to offer them to you. You also have a number of boxes here, old belongings. Do you want me to keep them?”

Explanation: Dad's a lawyer. Left my mother when I was twelve, for his receptionist. Terrible. In the cliché sense, but also in the lying, cheating, leaving-your-family-and-uprooting-in-nowhere, Nebraska sense. I hadn't seen him since my fourteenth birthday. No new kids, at least, so I don't have the *Replacement Family* baggage. Just, you know, a general massive void. He sends a text on my birthday that I don't return. That's about it.

“He's been married to Leslie for eleven years, Ma,” I reminded her. “I know. It's still shitty.”

“Well, that doesn't make her any less of a whore,” she said.

I sucked in a deep, deep breath, hissing it out like air from a balloon.

“I don't want the albums, but please hold onto the boxes for the time being, thank you,” I told her. “I'll come visit soon and take a look, see what I want to keep and get rid of. And maybe you should go and sit with Milly, next door. Have some coffee. We'll talk later."

I hung up, knowing entirely that we would not be talking later. I'd wait for her next call in a month.

Did I love my Mom? Of course. In a she-tried-her-broken-best sort of way. I'd long accepted her neurosis and penchant for nit-picking over every error I'd made since puberty. The acne: I didn't wash my face enough. Getting my period during gym class, in white shorts. Or pinching my stomach when I was fourteen and went through a period of rapid weight gain, blaming it on the doughnut shop across the street. I ate grapefruit and not much else during that season. Black coffee and a heaping spoonful of resentment.

Still, I know she loved me. In that desperate, I'm-sorry kind of way. I could tell, looking at her, that she knew how royally she had fucked up. The weight that constant criticism and insurmountable expectations can hang heavy on a developing girl. I ate grapefruit that one season during the weight gain, sure, but she also let me pick out the movies we'd watch on Wednesday nights: It Takes Two, *Three Men and a Baby*. She'd let me put whatever toppings I wanted on the popcorn. Or for my Bat Mitzvah, she bought me the most beautiful dress – garnet-colored, tea-length. I felt so dainty.

At my college graduation, she cried. It was captured in all the pictures. Blotting eyes, a truly proud smile.

Or when I got this job, exchanging our large house in New Jersey for a matchbox-sized apartment in LA: she gave me an extra-long hug at the airport and told me to be careful driving. That must count for something.

Still, I did struggle. I struggled with my self-image, perpetually feeling both frail and heavy, with love-handles and a belly that wouldn't shrink despite the detox teas I'd bought off Instagram, to my secret shame. I threw them out. Even if I had days where I didn't eat – in a time-crunch, for example, no actual reason – and my bones felt chalky, I'd catch myself in the mirror and grimace. Maybe my pants needed to be pulled up over my wide hips. Maybe my breasts were too big for the shirt I was wearing. I had not yet embraced a love for my curves, mother be damned.

I dragged myself into the shower and a pair of jeans, old concert T-Shirt, and mismatched socks. Charlie was home again, sitting on the kitchen counter, balancing a serving-bowl filled with cinnamon-raisin granola on his lap.

"I take it your date went well," I observed. "Or you passed out by the front door and I completely missed you, in which case I'm sorry."

"A bottle of blue Gatorade and tall glass of water, and I'm still dehydrated," he said. "I'm slowly getting my energy back, if that's any indicator. Yeah, it went well."

"You think you'll see them again?"

"They're coming over tomorrow, actually. We're going to watch the first season of *Mystery Science Theater* and I'm going to smoke a heinous amount of weed."

"Well, enjoy," I gave him a permissive wave. "I won't

be around later. I've got a thing to attend. God knows it's the last thing I feel like doing right now, though. My Mom called. One conversation with her is essentially the equivalent of a five-mile sprint. I think my limbs even hurt."

"I had an experience like that once, talking to my Dad," Charlie sympathized. "When I came out. And he went on and on questioning me about whether or not it was just a phase – you know, the usual. I told him I like sucking dick and fucking pussy and that was that. He didn't say anything after, except to remind my mother to get 2% milk at the store when she went out."

"You are literally the crudest person I know."

"It gets the point across," he said, setting the bowl in the sink. "Where are *you* supposed to go tonight? We both know I'm your only friend."

Okay, so sidebar: how I ended up here with Charlie, the twenty-three-year old barista with a BA in Literature from UCLA. Charlie, who spent the last year grinding coffee beans versus pursuing the occupation he'd worked so hard to earn a degree for. He'd tell you that he prefers the simple work. In and out. His parents wanted him to get that degree, but he just wanted to hang out and listen to old 2000's *Now That's What I Call Music* CDs in his bedroom.

I knew better, though. I knew it was a certain fear of leaving his comfort-bubble that was holding him back.

Still, when I moved to LA, I needed a roommate. I'd scored a good job with a decent starting salary, but I also had student loans. Old medical bills still hanging around from a kidney infection when I was seventeen. I had things to pay off. So I put an ad out on Craigslist, and Charlie showed up at my door, wearing a tie-dyed T-Shirt with a print of a pepperoni pizza slice, and we connected immediately over a love of cheap wholesale clothing and feeling bad about spending money on cheap wholesale clothing. You know, because of the working conditions and whatnot.

And that was that. The history of Charlie and I.

"A party in the Hills," I told him. "For that piece I'm working on."

"Elijah Mattox? You need to go," he insisted. "Go, and give me every delicious detail, or I'll pick out a dress and go myself. Please do it for those of us that have nothing better to do today than watch old Netflix reruns, I'm begging you."

"Fine," I exhaled loudly. "I'll go."

"Pictures!" Charlie yelled as I grabbed my purse and set course to find an appropriate dress. "I want to experience this vicariously through you. Take a shot every time you see a cock or someone whips their tits out. I love you."

"I love you, too," I groaned, slamming the door behind me.

Behind the door, I paused for a moment. The thought of the party, of that sexy feeling you get when you know you're gearing up to see a hot guy. The experience of it: washing, shaving every inch, painting your nails, putting on your makeup. Sliding that dress on. Slipping into a pair of heels. I tried to embrace it. I tried to push away any judgements on how my body looked, or how my complexion left a lot to be desired.

My heart stuttered. I decided to say fuck it, toss my insecurities to the wind, with Robyn's *Dancing on My Own* blaring. And I felt it, then – really felt it. Sexy. Inspired. Excited. Giddy, even. Jesus, had I ever used that word?

I danced at every stoplight. I let myself feel like the sensual, purposeful, driven woman that I was. Virgin or not. I was going to the party of someone who was technically an assignment, sure – but he wanted to see me, beautiful in a dress that was way out of my budget. Bold, daring, unexpectedly *Bailey*.

And it was, as Charlie would say, delicious.

"Well, fuck me."

Nothing makes you second-guess yourself like a room full of voluptuous models with tiny waists and breasts that still remained perky – side-boob abundant – without a bra. I told myself that if they were silicone, my boobs would look just as great in a thin, lacy bralette – but still found myself giving my own a mournful squeeze while hiding behind a potted plant. There there, boobs. You are stunning, even if you do fall sideways when I lie down. And one might be slightly bigger than the other. Spoiler alert: it was the left one. I'd named her Carly.

I'm still sexy, I told myself. I'm still *that* girl. *You go,*

Bailey.

When I tip-toed from behind my hiding spot, I was immediately hit by the blinding light of bleached-white smiles and perfectly-winged eyeliner. Glossy mouths, long faux eyelashes. Laughter that rang higher, almost melodic, alongside the beating music that was playing. I could feel my pulse rise; my brain determinedly running hurdles as I quickly looked around, trying to find a spot to belong in a room – nay, a house – brimming with men and women who looked like they belonged on the set of *Ex on the Beach*.

Or, you know, a porn set.

And then, *brain trip*. I think I went cross-eyed. Anxious, uncertain of myself, feeling like a mouse amongst sphinxes. One looked at me, then another, and I could tell what they were thinking: *who is this girl*? The girl in what now felt like an ill-fitting maroon-colored dress with a high-neckline and full-length sleeves. The girl who bought her makeup at Target and had never worn a single false eyelash, and had actually forgotten to put mascara on before leaving the house. *Who is she*?

And it wasn't in any sort of inspired way. A maybe-*she's-born-with-it* way. More like, who invited the walking tater tot? With no mascara, and practically blonde eyelashes, I suddenly felt as if I looked like a plague-ridden Victorian child.

You've made a massive mistake, the mean, DJ-sounding voice in my head informed. *Also, you're ugly*.

I waited restlessly for Eli to pop up, texting him that I had arrived, when one of the women approached me.

Pink-frosted hair, milky pale complexion – absolutely perfect, carved from ivory. Her highlighter made her cheeks pop; her eyes sparkled in that half-drunk, post-orgasm sort of way. She hadn't forgotten the mascara, and *oh*, how her ensemble was flawless. She was beautiful.

She smiled at me, almost too politely, and had the nerve to brush a strand of hair from my forehead.

"I've never seen you before," she remarked. "Have you worked with Eli?"

"Erm," I looked down at my knees. I felt, in that instant, like I had stumpy Hobbit legs. What was I thinking, wearing a dress that cut off mid-thigh? I should have gone for shorter; something to *elongate* my legs. And here I was. Dildo Baggins. "No. I work with *Come Magazine*. I've been interviewing him for an article."

"*Ah,*" she nodded. "That makes sense."

What was *that* supposed to mean? I could feel the Spanx sucking in my middle, wondering why the hell none of these women had an ounce of cellulite on them. Where were the actually curvy girls? Not to body-shame, of course – just for variety, for God's sake.

My face grew hot, and I had only just turned to walk straight out – sorry, Eli, another time, by which I mean a big fat NOPE – when he tapped me on the shoulder, extending a cocktail. The same he'd made me before.

"Morgan," he didn't take his eyes off me. I felt myself swallow, hard. He wore a fitted black button-down, black slacks, and a silver watch. His hair was purposefully messy. His smile cunning as ever. "This is my good friend, Bailey. Doesn't she look stunning?"

"Oh yes," Morgan agreed. "I love your shoes."

"Thanks," I told her. "Payless. Shoe Source."

She looked at me as if puzzled. Then, giving Eli a wide smile, she walked away and disappeared into the throw of glittery bodies.

"For the love of God," I exhaled heavily, relieved. I could hear Eli chuckle under his breath. "Could I just have some cake, please?"

He laughed louder, almost adoringly. As if he were charmed, and maybe he was. He left, returned with a big slice, and I happily accepted.

"I gave you a slice of the tip," he told me. "I wasn't sure if you were ready for the shaft, or into balls."

"I appreciate your consideration," I dug in, shoving a large spoonful into my mouth while the eyes of a hundred former *Miss-Carson-Cities* studied me like I was anything but a human woman. "It's all cake to me."

"I'm just happy you're enjoying yourself," he remarked. "I like a woman with a sweet tooth."

"It's more of a *whatever is on my plate* tooth," I said. "And I'm not enjoying myself. On the contrary, I feel like a walking raisin in need of a Xanax."

"What's wrong?" his expression fell, deeply concerned. "Did someone say something to you? Is it the music? I know, it's loud. I didn't pick it – it's the DJ's set."

"No," I said. "It's just, these women. I feel out of place here. Plus, I forgot to wear mascara."

For a second, I wanted to cry. I'm not sure why. I just felt entirely exposed and entirely out of place. And the worst bit – I was dubious of any singular reason that Elijah Mattox was standing next to me. What was it that he wanted? He had a penchant for fucking the women he worked with – and I, in a candid technicality, was someone he was working with.

"You look beautiful," he insisted gently. "Classy. En Vogue. Like Audrey Hepburn in *Breakfast at Tiffany's*."

"You are so full of shit," I smirked. "And how is it that you seem to have a movie reference for everything?"

Eli reached out, touching my chin, his head cocked slightly to the side.

"Bailey," he said softly. "I must tell you, I must admit: I've watched a lot of television."

I laughed, nudging him. For the time, we stood against a wall like we were both visitors – like he wasn't Elijah Mattox, or I some woman that was writing about him for a magazine – but two wallflowers. Two kids, standing awkwardly at the school dance, trading candy. Except our sweetness was in the banter. In the way his lips quirked. In the way his eyes, not just his voice, echoed laughter.

So, I said it:

"I want to be alone with you," I told him. "I don't want to fuck you, to be clear. I just want to talk. Unless you have others to attend to."

He shook his head, leading me swiftly to a quieter spot. Upstairs, in what looked like an office. A desk, a settee, a mahogany bookshelf that held volumes upon volumes of books, all stacked lazily atop one another. There was a photo of Eli, perhaps in his early-twenties, posing next to an older gentleman. They looked to be at a party. Another of he as a child, sitting in the grass, pulling up fistfuls of Dandelions. He was a toothy kid, with two front teeth that overlapped and eyes that seemed perpetually overjoyed for someone who also proclaimed himself to have been so very lonely.

"You wore braces, didn't you?" I said, turning to him. "Your teeth were crooked."

"Oh yeah," he said. "Twice, actually. Once when I was thirteen, and again in my mid-twenties. Invisalign is a great thing."

We both laughed lightly, sitting next to each other on the leather settee, suddenly silent.

"I was thinking," I told him. "Of doing a more extensive piece instead of the interview, if you were interested in something more comprehensive."

He scratched his neck, his eyebrows furrowed, pensive. "So, I'd be the focus? What would be the story?"

My skin prickled. I could feel my heart quicken – I was suddenly nervous, so nervous.

"Us," I replied, honestly. "Getting to know you, I guess? Getting to know all about you?"

"Getting to know you, getting to hope you like me?"

He sang the words, high-pitched, soft. We both laughed.

"How many times have you seen *The Sound of*

Music?" I asked him. "This is off the record."

"Oh, keep it on the record," he said. "Twelve. Julie Andrews is an icon."

"I always skipped the ending," I said. "Too sad."

Eli nodded.

"You know what?" he said. "Me too. I've never seen the whole film. Twelve times, and I've never watched the ending."

We both looked at each other, locked-in, mutually intrigued by this shared morsel of childhood information.

"We should watch it together sometimes," I said.

"I'd like that," he said. "You are certainly my cup of tea."

The room smelled of clove. Of vague cigar and Eli's cologne. We were inches apart, then separated only by a fingertip.

"It's hard for me to believe that," I found myself whispering.

"Why?" he asked, truly astounded, it seemed.

"I've never been anyone's cup of tea," I told him. "Just my own."

"I think that's wonderful," he said. He smiled, warm and kind. "Can I kiss you?"

"What?" I think I asked. I barely made a sound. "Kiss me?"

He nodded. I nodded. The room spun.

Eli leaned in and kissed me. One kiss, soft as a petal, then another, more aggressive, yet restrained. His mouth tasting like nothing but himself and maybe a hint of alcohol.

I raised a hand to his face, caressing his cheek, and he did the same. Our noses touched, our eyes barely open, completely stolen by the moment.

We kissed again, breathless. Suddenly closer, molded together, arms wrapping. The noises soft, muffled by our mouths; our collective breathing both sharp and shallow.

When we pulled apart, the air stilled.

"You are a very good kisser," was all I could say. My heart stumbled. "That was a new experience."

"You don't say?" he poked my nose sweetly, leaning back. He brushed the hair from his eyes, his cheeks pinched pink. He looked younger, more boyish, his smirk elven.

"You know, you should visit me on set," he suggested. "You could see me work. If you felt comfortable, that is. More substance for the article."

My mind was still running slow from the kiss. My brain hazy, my mouth still slightly agape.

Visit him on set? Watch him fuck some strange woman? Well, a stranger to me. They were all strangers to me. Was that a normal thing to ask a girl, especially after kissing her? After a *room-spinning* kind of kiss.

Did he really like me, or was this just a kiss?

Suddenly, I drifted back into myself. Poised, slowly regaining posture. I sat up a bit straighter, taking a small breath.

"Sure," I said, feeling a sudden pang of disheartenment. "Just give me an address, and I'll be there."

CHAPTER 4
On-Set Fuckery of the Literal Kind

I was mid-way through shoving a forkful of admittedly sad-looking, wilted Caesar salad (I'd gone heavy on the dressing) into my mouth, when my phone buzzed.

I gave it a glance, sighing.

Elijah: *I'll be on set at 3. Arrive a half hour earlier or so if you want to chat beforehand.*

He texted me the address. I took a second before replying: *OK*. Two letters.

I felt a sudden, inexplicable stillness then. I wasn't entirely sure why. I wasn't sure why I suddenly cared so much about the kiss, or Eli, or whether or not I was special in some regard. But for some reason, the thought of watching Eli fuck on-set halted me; even my train-of-thought had paused.

"Adam," I said, beckoning Deborah's assistant. "Adam!"

"What's up?" he asked, poking his head around the cubicle corner. "Shit. You look exhausted."

"Could you get Deborah for me?" I asked. "I'm having a moment of apathy and can't bring myself to move."

"Yikes," he muttered, eyebrows raised in quaint concern. "Sure thing."

She appeared moments later, forever the sudden

apparition in dark lipstick and perfectly hair-sprayed tresses. Her stilettos looked particularly painful.

"Yes, dear?" she asked, letting herself in. She sat down on the lumpy crescent-shaped chair that had existed since probably forever, and had moved about between cubicles. It was torn in corners; the fabric a faded shade of Persimmon. "Adam told me you looked as if in crisis. Are you ill?"

"Deb," I sighed again, looking at her. "Am I special?"

Her expression shifted: concerned, surprised, and then gentle – motherly, caring, soft.

"Oh, honey," she said gently. "Of course you're special. You're brilliant. The idea you had, turning the interview into a full story piece? Brilliant. And your first piece, to boot."

I'd emailed her the idea the night before, and she'd responded almost immediately, solely in exclamation points.

"Elijah wants me to visit him on set," I told her. "What do I do, just stand there and watch him fuck?"

Her face lit up, throwing her hands up, suddenly bemused.

"Yes! You must go!" she insisted, pulling me up from my chair. It was a drawn-out affair, since I was essentially a lump of clay without working legs. I teetered on my own two feet as I stood. "Go, and watch him fuck – get an actual look into what he does. Then talk to him about it. Maybe get yourself a green juice, too. You look like you're lacking vitamins."

"It's all the Red Bull," I confessed. "Deb, I haven't had water in like two weeks."

Suddenly, my throat swelled. My face grew hot. It was utterly perplexing. Deborah hugged me tightly, and against her bosom I could smell her perfume – lilac, bergamot.

"He kissed me," I said, directly into her blouse. "I think I like him."

She pulled away, looking straight at me, shocked.

"At the party?" she asked.

"Yeah," I told her. "Except I don't think I'm all that special. I feel like a fucking teenager. *Special*? Are you kidding me? Next I'll be writing a note asking him to check a box if he likes me or not."

"What happened, exactly?"

"We kissed, and then immediately after he'd mentioned this thing about me visiting him on set. Which I don't know, makes me think that if he's so casual with the thought of me watching him fuck someone else, he mustn't be that into me."

"Baby doll," she said softly. "It's just his job. You've known that."

"Yeah," I exhaled, crestfallen. "He's just been very candid about how much he enjoys it."

"Well sure," Deborah agreed. "He's getting laid. I'm sure he does enjoy it. I'd enjoy a slice of what he gets to do every day. Maybe just once. I'm imagining a buff, Liam Neilson-looking type. I'm his Psychiatrist, and he's the patient, and he takes me on my desk, bareback."

"Good fucking lord," I exclaimed. "Fine. I think I'll

head over now."

"Bailey," she added as I grabbed my bag, slinging it over a shoulder. "It's just sex. Don't think too much about it."

Says the minx to the virgin. The mean-DJ voice in my head took ahold of his microphone: *Bailey Finch, congratulations, you are juvenile. Do you want a juice box to go with that terrible tween attitude of yours? Also, you're gross.*

"I'll try," I said to her. "Who knows, maybe I'll enjoy watching him fuck. I know you'd love that."

"I'll need all the details, obviously. Write as you watch," she grinned. "And Bailey, if you're looking for a guy, this isn't him. That's all I'll say. I'm not saying he's out of your *league*, but you're a straight-forward girl. You're sweet. And the lifestyle of a porn star is anything but straightforward."

"Or maybe it is straightforward," I remarked. "Straight-forwarding his dick into someone's vagina, or mouth, or..."

"*Go,*" she commanded. "Save the dating game for your apps or Trivia Nights at Applebee's. Focus on the article now. Go, watch this guy fuck, and seriously, have a green juice after."

"I'm on it," I told her. "Not literally. Even if I do kind of want to be on *it*. His dick, I mean."

I flushed at my own admission, actually able to laugh at myself. Feeling a little lighter, a little more in-control.

As I left, skirting through the parking lot, I took a second to really think about it: yeah, I liked this guy. I think he liked me, too. I really did. But even if he *did*, I wasn't the type of girl to get involved with a porn star.

Not that I knew what type of girl was right for a porn star, that is. Maybe another porn star. Or maybe someone like me. But just not me, in particular. There would never a Bailey + Elijah on some tabloid cover. There was no name combo in store for us. What would that even look like? *Bai-li*? That feels sweepingly inappropriate.

To quote the parlance of my generation: *that's the tea, sis*.

With LA traffic per usual, I showed up about a half hour late. This wouldn't have been a problem, except by the time of my arrival, there was no one in the lobby apart from the security guard – a young guy with an impressive mustache – to greet me.

"I have no idea where I'm supposed to go," I told him. For profession sake, I flashed my *Come Magazine* badge. "Where is Elijah Mattox shooting?"

"Ah," he nodded, as of he'd answered this question a million times before, and maybe he had. "Down the hall, at the far end, and he'll be in the room on your first right. You'll see it. Hell, you'll probably hear him."

He walked away, laughing wittingly, to answer another call. I took his directions and guardedly navigated through the brightly-lit hallway, the walls adorned with framed photos of various adult film starlets. I tried to see if I could recognize any of them from the party. I stopped at each, giving a good squint. And, there she was.

Morgan. Bare-breasted, heavily airbrushed, holding two cocks at once, looking deliberately perplexed: as in, which one should I suck? Her eyes were playful, heavily-lined, her mouth slick with gloss. Her whole body, barely clad except for a neon-pink thong, was covered in a wet-like sheen. Baby oil, maybe. Photoshop, probably.

I sucked in a deep breath and continued on until I reached the far end of the hall, the first right.

The first thing I noticed was the distinct, almost excessive moans coming from behind the door. They were a woman's. I didn't hear Eli.

But when I opened the door, sneaking in quietly, I saw him. In all his naked glory, his hair a sweaty mess, fucking the life out of a stick-figure of a girl on a bare mattress. The room was dimly lit, grim in its gray-bathed walls and cement floor. Prison-like. There were fake windows with bars, and some unknown pool of liquid on the floor. I didn't want to guess what it was.

"Oh, fuck me!" she cried out, grabbing his hair. He fucked her harder, deeper, a look of concentration on his face as he thrust – in and out – rhythmically, in a way that looked almost painful. "Oh, oh..."

He panted like a dog, the breadth of his body tensing. I could see every inch of him – sinewy, his muscles taut. He gleamed, occasionally sprayed down with water, his moans more subtle, authentic. I'm sure they were.

"I knew you wanted it like this when I first saw you. Sitting there, on the park bench, practically begging for me to take you," his tone husky, rigid. "I'm going to send you back to school, covered in cum. And if you tell anyone, I'll kill you."

"No," she begged. "Please don't. Cum inside me instead. Please. Please!"

He struck her, straight across the face, hard. My stomach dropped.

"Shut the fuck up," his voice was hoarse, cut like broken glass. "Shut your fucking mouth. I'll cum wherever I want, as many times as I want. Do you understand?"

His hands grabbed her throat, his fingers wrapping around. I could see her face turn a shade blue, her arms going limp, her eyes widening.

Was she breathing? God, was she breathing?

I could feel my skin go hot, my chest constricting. My body was a single, tightened cord. As he pulled out, jacking himself off all over her face, hair, tits, I felt a mix of disgust and arousal. An ache between my legs, and the taste of bile in my mouth.

When the act was finished, the director cut through with a swift: "Good! Good. Excellent. I think we've got it."

Both Eli and the woman were suddenly bright, pleasantly congenial. The room was filled with a burst of warmth as the set walls were moved, exposing more light.

He grabbed her a damp towel, cleaned her off

carefully. His touch was delicate, light, as he brushed her hair back with gentle fingertips and asked for another clean towel. She told him she was going to shower, anyway. He tossed the towel playfully at her legs.

"You never let me help!" he jokingly accused. "Heaven forbid."

They laughed. They hung their arms around each other like old friends. She then grabbed one of the towels, lazily wrapped it around her torso, and disappeared into another room. Eli shook his head, collected himself, and asked for a bottled water. Then he glanced around, scanning the room. I was carefully hidden behind a prop, and I wondered if he was looking for me. Wondering if I'd bothered to show.

I still felt the sour taste in my mouth, the confusion, the ache. A sudden dizziness.

Quickly, I dipped out before I was seen, finding the nearest bathroom. My face was pallor, my mouth slack.

I locked myself in a bathroom stall, my head spinning, my heart racing, and took in a deep breath. A marrow-deep shiver crept up my spine.

And sliding my fingers between my legs, I touched myself. Softly, gently, above the fabric of my corduroy skirt. Then, hiking it up, I slid my panties aside and touched my clit, a gentle button press. I stroked progressively faster, occasionally dipping into my wet slit, until I felt it – a rush of blood to the head, the swift contraction – like a drug, spreading quickly throughout my whole body, then dissipating.

I panted softly, my brow damp, my body trembling slightly. When I exited the stall, I gave a silent thanks that no one was there to hear me. The weirdo masturbating in a public bathroom. But hey, it was a thing.

I wiped my face down with a wet paper towel, and checked myself again. My cheeks had reddened, the color returned to my mouth. A straight pink line.

There was almost a feeling of embarrassment, having seen him fuck. I wanted to see him again, but I also wanted to get the hell out of there before he saw me, and pretend I hadn't come. Nope, I missed it. Last-minute meeting. You know how it is.

I found him in the lobby, sitting on one of the sofas, having a fruit juice. He was, blessedly, fully clothed. He looked like he'd cleaned up, showered, even shaved.

When he saw me, he perked up, smiling broadly. I wasn't sure what the hell to say.

"Where did you get that juice?" I asked. "I'm in need of more B12."

He stood, his T-shirt somehow molding to his body magnificently, motioning me to follow him. Down another short corridor, there was a smoothie bar. I ordered a green juice – kale, spinach, apples, cucumber, mint – and sipped it quietly. Eli studied me with the intensity of a schoolboy last-minute cramming for a test.

"You're thirsty," he noted. "Your face is flush."

"It's hot in here," I told him. "I think your AC is broken."

He nodded.

"Did you show up late?"

I hesitated, pressing my lips together on the plastic straw. I wanted to make a passive comment about how they were bad for the environment, but deciding that this was less clever and more gratingly obnoxious, I just said:

"I showed up while you were mid-fucking," I informed him. "Or maybe it was more towards the tail-end. I'm not sure. Well done."

"Yeah?" he seemed amused. "Is that how you really feel?"

"Would you prefer I feel something different?" I asked him. "Do you want me to feel jealous?"

I meant it lightly, as more of a joke. But he appeared to think I was serious.

"Not at all," he said. "But it's normal to feel something."

We looked at each other, knowingly. He looked so sweet, standing there, in the hallway of a porn studio.

"I think you're very interesting," I admitted.

He smiled, sincere and small.

"I like you too," he said. "Bailey Finch. Do you want to get dinner with me some time? Off the record."

Here it was: Elijah Mattox, asking me out to dinner. Did I want to? Yes. Yes, absolutely – but also no, not at all. Never. We weren't the match I wanted us to be. Even if I had masturbated with the ferocity of a teenage boy's first time, in a bathroom stall.

I still felt a tinge of nausea, too. I mean, they didn't use a condom, even. I knew of the extensive tests, the transparency, that it was all an act. But still.

Could I date someone that was so exceedingly exposed? Did I even want that, or was I just physically attracted to him? People get crushes all the time. It didn't have to mean anything if I didn't want it to.

"I don't know," I said, honestly. "Can I take the night to think about it?"

His eyes softened, visibly disappointed.

"I understand. Professional conflict," he said. But it wasn't professional conflict. It was personal. "As you wish."

Oh, my timid heart.

"Was that a *Princess Bride* reference?" I was elated. "Or am I hearing things?"

He grinned, boyishly, nodding.

"Well," I said. "Even if that was – well, honestly, perfect timing, and probably my most beloved film – I'm still taking the night to think about it. It's not for professional reasons. It's personal."

"So you *do* like me?" he teased, beaming. "Oh, happy day."

"Don't be abrasive," I told him, turning sharply. "Or I'll write that you sweat profusely in your scenes, and it's not attractive."

He laughed loudly, and I spun around, feeling his eyes follow me out the door.

"As you wish!" I heard him exclaim. My heart sprouted wings.

Outside the door, the heat causing a buzz in the air, I smiled. Sure, I liked him. But I was also so, so confused.

Virgin stuff. Porn star stuff. Professional stuff, compatibility stuff. All of the stuff.

Traffic en-route home was just as bad. I watched the clouds drift like floating gauze across a milky-pink sky. Music blared through open windows, horns honked, brakes screeched. Still, there was a musical essence to it all.

I turned up the radio, Justin Timberlake's *Cry Me A River*, and sang along.

Things you don't do when conflicted: deep internet dives.

Painting the scene: exactly 1:32am. I'm a sleeping bag, complete with hood, rolled up like a bright orange glow-worm, with my laptop open.

Charlie knocked, peeking his head in.

"Why in God's name are you awake?" he asked, dubious. "Why are you wearing a sleeping bag?"

"I'm immersed in a deep internet dive."

"Elijah Mattox," he eye-rolled. "That's a terrible idea, and you know it."

It was. It so terribly was. I threw a pillow at him, and he shut the door, yelling once more through the cheap over-painted plank of plywood that guarded my bedroom: "It's a terrible idea, Bailey. Watch cat videos instead. You love those. Or go on Tumblr and look at old pictures of Cher."

I didn't listen, because of course I didn't. Instead, I

dove. I dove deep. I watched approximately two hours of scenes – how many that accounted for, I couldn't count.

I searched for the softer stuff first. Scant findings: a few in a mansion's room, with intricately-woven bedding and silk, red sheets. She was his mistress. He fucked her tenderly, in long strokes, kissing her with an open mouth. Another in a bathroom, with the same woman, in a shower. He had her bent over the bath, fucking her from behind, their bodies drenched. He kissed her after he came, passionately.

My stomach fell. When it ended, I searched for the harder scenes.

There was a scene where Eli played a Head Master who was fucking two identical-twins students who looked young. Age-play. One sucked his cock while the other sucked his balls, his hands grabbing their hair, pulling. He fucked one on the desk while the other watched, touching herself. Another scene: a dungeon, rusted chains on the floor, while he fucked a naked woman with hair that looked as if combed by a rake, on the bare ground. She squirmed and cried as he fucked her, harder and harder, his voice harsh as he told her to shut her mouth.

Another clip: a woman's head under water, while he fucked her, his hand holding her down by the hair. He came all over her back. Another, fucking a woman while a noose was tied around her neck, tightening, tightening...he released the noose, her body falling to the floor. Then he fucked her ass while she cried out for more, clawing her hands on the floor, her expression pained. He pulled out before he came. There was cum everywhere. All over her mouth, her stomach (all abs), her chest. It was in her hair. He breathed raggedly, looking like a caged animal.

I felt the bile in my mouth again. I tried a few deep breaths, wiping the hair from my eyes, immediately filled with regret.

I squeezed my eyes shut, trying to remember the human, Elijah Mattox. The sweet man who quoted *The Princess Bride* and sang along to *the Sound of Music*.

And yet I couldn't. I was already past that point – the bridge has been burned. It was then I wondered if he had seen *Phantom of the Opera*, and oh, I'm sure he had, because he was so painfully compatible in areas of interest.

Still, that's not everything.

I shut my laptop, enclosed in the dark and the soft plush of my sleeping back, laying atop my bed. I squirmed out of the bag and pushed it off the side, then crawled beneath my covers.

What the fuck had I just done?

I lay there, quiet, the fan humming erratically. The damn thing spun as if it were ready to fall from the ceiling.

Perhaps this was better. It would be easier for me to keep it professional. Feelings needed to be off the table. It should have been that way from the get-go.

So I tried to sleep. I slept, fitfully, wracked with dreams of hard fucking and hair pulling. Of things I hadn't even experienced. I woke up, still feeling a slight pain in my chest. Still panged with regret.

There was one missed call: Eli. I didn't return it. I would email him from the office on Monday, as the correspondence should remain.

CHAPTER 5
Does Ignoring People Count as a Resume Skill?

I ignored Elijah for two straight weeks. In that time:
Twenty-three texts.
Ten phone-calls.
Eight voicemails.
On the last two calls, he didn't bother leaving a message. I didn't even reply to his emails. And when he went the route of contacting Deborah, insisting his attempts were in relation to *my* professional endeavors, I really took the high road:
I called out of work.
"Darling," Deborah paused. From over the phone, I could hear the acrylic tap of her nails against a glass desk. Faint keyboard sounds chirped in the background. "As you've yet to take a vacation or sick day since you started here, I'll allow you a week to figure out whatever this nonsense is with Elijah Mattox."
"I'm serious, Deb," I faked a muffled cough. It was utterly unconvincing. "I think it's strep. Maybe it's the measles. It's all these unvaccinated kids, Deborah. I'm on my way to the ER. My Lyft is like, two minutes away."
From outside my bedroom, Charlie was playing against himself in a very tense game of Wii Sports. I could hear the sounds of his muttering under his breath;

the controller inevitably flying from his hand, straight into the television screen.

"You stupid whore!" he yelled.

"Charlie!" I put the phone to my shoulder. "You know how I feel about the W word in this house."

"I was talking about MYSELF."

He stormed around. I could hear the heavy footsteps of his sulky mad-boy theatrics thump around the living room. A heavy sigh. Keys jangling. Then, the front door opened and closed. He had left.

I wondered briefly if there was something else going on.

"Bailey," Deborah's voice was muted by my shoulder. Shit. "Are you there? This fucking phone system. Someone call Adam. Tell him to call the powers that be at Cisco and tell them to piss off."

"No," I snapped back, somehow winded. "Deb, I'm here. I'm here. I'm just exhausted."

"Take a beat, then," she said, sincere and understanding, which was completely unbelievable considering how I could barely even pay attention to the conversation. "Take a nap. Take a lot of naps. Eat some greens. And call that boy. I want this project to continue smoothly."

My heart stretched. Everything – my limbs, my brain – felt heavy as lead.

"Yeah," I mumbled. "I'll call him. I promise, Deb."

"Good. It's been four minutes. You're running late for your Lyft."

Click.

So yeah, she gave me the time off. I could have accomplished a lot with that time, too. I could have written another piece. I could have started a novel, even. I could have goddamn journaled. I could have even made a vision board. I had enough magazines strewn under my bed.

But I was in such a funk, I didn't. I ordered McDonalds via Postmates and drank the leftover powdered Kool-Aid that Charlie had bought months ago when he wanted to try and dye his hair red. Instead of this being a period of functional activity, it was sheer fucking passivity. If I had seen the whole thing unfold as an outsider, I would have shaken myself.

It was only when the Kool-Aid container was empty and I couldn't stomach another McDouble that I decided to wash my hair, put on a pair of actual pants, and take a walk. The weather was nice enough – cool, but not deceptively so. Not the sort of temperate coolness that quickly disappears after you've walked a block. By the end of it, you're panting and you've practically shed all your clothes. You're wearing a cami that's just sheer enough to broadcast the new bra you had no intention of broadcasting to the friendly neighborhood – because you'd thought it was *just cool enough* to wear a sweatshirt.

Even my internal monologue was exhausting.

It wasn't a long walk; just around the building. I watched the children play in the small playground reserved just for the tenants. I tried to not immediately think of Elijah fucking some model immediately after. I watched a Shiba puppy trot happily ahead of his owner, tail wagging, and tried to suppress the thought of Elijah choking some raven-haired actress name Lianna Park until her face turned white.

Cum. So much cum. Everywhere. What do these women think about needing to constantly wash that shit out of their hair?

Finally, I sat down on the pavement, flat in the middle of the parking lot. It was afternoon. It was empty enough. And I tried to ignore the pebbles under my butt, of which my leggings didn't serve as a particularly great barrier. I tried to focus on my breathing, of being in the present, attempting a moment of Zen.

I closed my eyes, and saw Elijah's face. A soft smile. A gently-mouthed *hi*.

I pictured him drinking a coffee, in plain clothes, squinting at a New York Times article. I imagined him at the gym, lifting, his breath heavy, sweat trickling down his brow. I imagined him grocery shopping alone, rolling a rickety-cart along the produce aisles of avocados and oranges and lemons, carefully selecting one, examining, then placing it back. I imagined him eating Poptarts in the morning, making faces at himself while in the mirror while he shaved, singing along to his favorite song. I reminded myself that there was so much more to him.

Elijah Mattox: Full-Time Human.

My phone buzzed, rattling against the pavement. I glanced over.

It was Eli.

I didn't pick up.

Rewinding a bit: I had one last interview to conduct, an additional last-minute coverage assignment, helping out a colleague with food poisoning, before I was technically able to take my sabbatical. Her name was Fleur Ross: an Instagram and YouTube Influencer who had just reached ten-million subscribers. She had now written a book, poised to be a best-seller, no doubt, and here I was.

Her house was cozier than I had envisioned. I figured it would be more sterile: white walls, minimalistic furnishings and artwork. Maybe a splash of color through an Orchid placed on a mantle – but it was a far cry from that. Fleur's home was almost cottage-like. The walls were covered with all sorts of artwork; the frames in various sizes and colors – bronze, silver, hot pink. She was either a painter or a fan of paintings. There was also a mess of photography lazily tacked on the walls. Her stone fireplace just barely flickered, kept alive on its last embers.

As I sat on the couch, waiting for her to make tea (she was putting on the kettle, she had said) I squinted at the photographs. She looked young in them; with friends, with family. There was a dog that I didn't see existed here, in this house. Her 10-million subscriber plaque from YouTube rested on a bookshelf, almost hidden in-between a thick stack of magazines and books.

She was not at all, at least in this space, what I had imagined.

"Is lemongrass tea alright with you, Bailey?" she called from the kitchen. I could hear the kettle hiss. Her accent was airy, Midwestern, soft as cotton. "It's all I've got, I'm afraid. Unless you want instant. I think I have a tin of Lipton around here somewhere. Oh, shit."

There was a rattle of pots and pans as she – I could only assume – was searching for cups. I tapped a finger on the arm-rest, my laptop open next to me. The couch – royal purple, velvet, and so plush that I nearly sank into it – was covered in cat hair. I could see the cat snoozing in the corner, by the aforementioned bookcase. It was a very fat, orange tabby cat. It purred loudly, unphased by the racket in the kitchen. I could feel my allergies kick in – sneeze, wipe nose on my sleeve, cringe at the fact that I had wiped my nose on my sleeve.

Fleur came out with the tea in dainty tea-cups, set atop a silver tray. She set it down on a coffee table that wavered clumsily beneath the weight. I picked up the tea and sipped with a slight hesitancy as she sank down in the chair across from me. It was equally as plush as the sofa, upholstered in a dusty-rose fabric, with the stitching loose in spots.

She cocked her head to the side as she watched me, her smile wide. I had the terrible thought – or perhaps it wasn't so terrible – that I noticed the collagen. Lip injections. I had a knack for picking out plastic surgery on a face.

"It's pretty incredible," I decided to start, picking up

my laptop, nestling it on my lap. "Ten-million. You hit that number in what, two weeks?"

"Twelve days," she corrected. "Who knew people would be so interested in learning about how not spend a shit-ton of money on drive-thru coffee, or how to make origami animals out of toilet paper?"

"So you'd consider yourself sort of a life-hack coach?" I mused. "Helping the youth save money, while being crafty."

"I suppose," she said. "You want to know how it all started? I learned the origami thing during high-school. I wasn't exactly popular. I was missing teeth from lack of childhood dental care and I walked with a limp. Anyway, this guy poured an entire 2 liter bottle of Sprite into my backpack, and so I punched him, square in the nose. Broke it. They suspended me for two weeks, and I legit had nothing better to do at home than start playing with the damn toilet paper."

She nestled deeper into the chair. She gave me a satisfied smile, flashing a mouthful of pearly white, perfectly straight, perfectly carved veneers. No more missing teeth for Fleur.

It was astounding, really. Here she was – immaculately dressed, even if it was a little eccentric. Her gray blouse had puff sleeves, a wide collar, unbuttoned to reveal a peek at her clavicle. Hanging on the chain of her necklace was a tiny gold cat. Her pants were tissue-paper thin, and I could see her underwear beneath the white, weathered fabric. Red panties. They matched her lipstick. And she – Fleur, this woman –

spoke so sweetly. How could anyone pour a bottle of soda into her backpack?

"That's horrible," I remarked. "I'm so sorry that happened to you."

"You want to know the funniest bit about it?" she quipped. "I eventually lost my virginity to that guy. I was working at one of those corner markets that sells hardly anything except for those mini powdered donuts and One Hour Energy shots. He came in, bought a pack of Twix, and then fucked me in the stock room."

I was stunned. Utterly stunned.

"And you wanted that?" I spurted. "I mean – I'm sorry – I don't mean that in any kind of condescending way. But, I mean, did you *want* to lose your virginity like that?"

She paused, mulling it over, sipping her tea in a sort of casual way. As if I'd asked about her thoughts on changing the color scheme of her bathroom. What colored paint? What sort of wallpaper print?

"Yeah," she nodded. "I'd say so. After it was over, the boy was terribly flushed. Panting. When he pulled his pants up, he kissed me in a very tender way. He told me, *I always thought you were cute, with the limp. I'm sorry about the Sprite.* He bought me a pack of Juicy Fruit and left."

"Did you ever see him again?"

"Eh," she shrugged. "Once or twice. He's married now, with a baby. Looks just like him. I don't think about it much these days, except for the occasional bout of gratitude that will occasionally sweep over me. I mean, if not for the soda/backpack incident of 2009, I wouldn't be here."

"I suppose that's true."

She nodded. "I did cut him a check once. When I found out he was getting married, I sent him a card. That wedding gift probably paid for the down-payment on his mortgage."

I was typing slowly, my lips pursed.

"And so you've written a book," I decided to change the subject. "About thriving amidst the daily chaos of life. Life-hacks, as I'd mentioned, but with a broader purpose. That's quite a topic to tackle."

"For sure," she agreed. "But it's something we all face, every day. I couldn't even buy a cup of coffee without wading through a line of people who seemed miserable to simply be conscious. And we've got to move past that. Just today, you know, I saw a guy pissing on the front steps of an apartment building. Literally, fly down, pissing on the brick. How do you deal with that?"

"And you started off pretty humbly in terms of living circumstances," I said, and it was true. I had read the articles, of which there were many. "Single mom, five brothers."

"Food stamps, housing assistance. Yeah," she said. "Thus begins the kind of girl that would eventually toy around with bathroom products. The inspiration for one of the chapters in my book came from one of my mother's exes. He'd thrown a television remote, and it hit the window. Totally shattered the glass everywhere.

Anyway, I picked up all of the bigger pieces and made artwork with it. Painted the glass. Tried to fit it together, like a puzzle. It's hanging in my pantry."

Her candor was astounding. I liked to think that I was pretty blunt, and maybe I was, but this kind of poised vulnerability struck me in a very moving way. Maybe it's because I had my own family bullshit. I used to be fat, and now I'm less fat, but still fat, and even though I'm happy, my mother will still call me out on it. One Hanukkah, she made me eat stir-fried vegetables from the steamer-bag while my father had potato pancakes, smothered in salt and oil.

"Is it hard, to be so honest?" I asked her.

"Sometimes," she confessed. "What's harder is once you make a career out of being vulnerable, you really need to start checking yourself. And I mean constantly. You question what's candid, and what's for the camera. What's *real,* I guess. So every morning, I have some quiet time to myself. Before I do anything else – brush my teeth, eat breakfast, look at my phone – I do some deep breathing, and try to center myself."

"And that works?"

"Not always, but usually," she said. "Has honesty always come easily to you?"

"God, no," I told her. "I mean, well, yes and no. I'm fine with talking about some things, but not others. And I have to really click with the people I talk to about personal stuff. Right now I'm dealing with that, actually."

"Yeah?" Fleur leaned forward, setting her cup aside.

She stroked her thighs, as if petting the cat that still dozed in the corner. Still purring. "Care to share?"

"Well..." I sucked in a deep breath. "There's a guy I like. We haven't gone on an official date or anything, but we've seen each other around. We've made out. Only..."

I paused, sucked in another breath. I was trying to be as honest as I could without giving any details that would jeopardize my piece. We had a very lips-sealed practice when it came to publications. At least, with anyone outside of the bubble.

"...only, I've never had sex. That feels so weird to say out loud at my age. I'm twenty-four. And this guy, he's experienced. He's also in way better shape than I am. No interesting rolls whatsoever."

I expected a more extravagant reaction. A gasp, or jazz hands.

Instead, she shrugged.

"Just tell him," she said, simple as that. "It really doesn't matter. Just tell him. Either he's fine with it, or he's not. It's one of those terrible cliche's, really. If it's meant to be, it's meant to be. A word of advice, though: lube. Lots of it."

"Will do," I muttered, fingers scanning the keyboard. "I'll make a note: Astroglide."

"And Bailey," she said. "Remember, you're not a commodity. People aren't things. He should want you for who you are, not just your vagina. You'll figure it out."

When the interview was over, I sent my notes over to Deborah, and decided that yes, I was going to do it. Be vulnerable. Tell Elijah straight-up what was going on.

And that way, we could work together without all of the bullshit baggage we had somehow seemed to accumulate in the span of no freaking time whatsoever.

I was in such a state that I didn't notice the car in his driveway when I pulled up. The gate, to my surprise, was still open. It shut behind me, as if sealing me in. This was going to happen. Maybe even *it* would happen. Was I ready for that? Was *it* what I wanted?

I knocked on the door, and there was a long pause before he answered. I spent a solid five minutes examining the manicured shrubbery that crept around the parameter of his stucco castle.

When he answered, he seemed shocked, unnerved. He seemed almost off-balance, wavering slightly as he stood there in his boxers, and nothing else.

"Bailey," he stammered. "Now's not a good time. Can I call you later?"

"Why?" I asked, suddenly caring. Suddenly caring so much. "Do you have just a minute? I just really, *really* want to talk to you about something. It's kind of ridiculous, it's – um..."

"Bailey," he interrupted. Stern. "Not now, okay? I'm really sorry. I'll call you tonight, though. I promise. We can get dinner."

It was then that I heard her. Her voice was an adorable, airy sound; half-way between a child and woman's. She had the voice of an actress from vintage films of the past, if that meant anything.

"Eli," she called from another room. "Eli, the ice machine is making a weird sound. You should probably look at it."

She peered from around the corner, dressed in nothing but her bra and panties, her hair in a frazzled state. It was only then, upon examining the subtleties in Elijah's face – the slight rouge, the flush of his lips, the way he breathed quavered slightly.

My heart fell to my feet.

"Did you fuck her?" I asked. "Like, just now?"

"Bailey," he started.

"I don't see any cameramen anywhere," I remarked. "Is this for a shoot?"

"Bailey," he repeated, almost desperate. "Please go home. I'll call you later."

"Go?" It came out as a choke. I didn't mean it to. And then, creeping over me like vines over broken brick-work, there was the anger. "You go. You go fuck yourself. Hell, you go and fuck whoever she is again. I don't care. Whoop-di-fucking-doo."

I stormed off, hating myself for what I'd said, crying as I got into my car and slammed the door, driving off. It was all a blur. The entire conversation. My feelings. The entire large two-topping pizza I consumed immediately after, all by myself, sitting in the restaurant like a sad divorcée.

I thought about Eli. I thought about the project. I thought about how badly all of this hurt, and he hadn't even managed to get me out of *my* clothes. It was all so surface-level and yet sliced so deep.

I needed to go somewhere. I needed to get out of my head.

I texted Charlie: *We're going out. Wear your mesh top and take an Ibuprofen. We're getting lit tonight.*

CHAPTER 6
Hot Tip: Don't Smoke Crack

On record, this was probably one of the poorest decisions I could have made. I was not the clubbing type. I wasn't even the drinking type. And as a journalist, who was technically on sabbatical, and who should have instead been preoccupied learning the *Art of Tidying Up* or perusing articles on Gawker while inhaling a pint of Talenti, it was the poorest goddamn move I could have possibly ever, ever made.

But that's what we do, don't we? Growing up is such a mindfuck. One moment, you've got it together – you're balancing your bank account, you've got Excel spreadsheets tracking every penny of your budget, and you seriously consider interest rates.

Then, nosedive. You're three sheets to the wind, shirt up over your head, tits out, dancing on a bar table while the horrified bartender contemplates calling the cops. You then proceed to hook up with the very same bartender later that night, and the Walk of Shame home is not nearly as cute or comical as they make it look in the movies. You have a headache. There's a trash-can person pissing off the edge of the street.

And so here I was, diving right into the thick of things – all because I wanted to forget about a stupid boy that I barely knew. It was a *crush*, for God's sake. All we had done was made out, and I ghosted him because he fucked women for a living, which I knew going into the whole damn thing.

God, this is getting long-winded. I'm sorry.

So I texted Charlie, sitting in my car, double-fisting a bag of two large McDonald's french fries. When he responded, my fingers, covered in grease, couldn't unlock the phone with my fingerprint. That, that one minuscule thing, was almost enough to make me sob.

He called, and I picked up.

"Did you get grease on your phone again? Get it together, woman."

"You know me," I said. "Take me somewhere sleazy tonight."

I could feel him grinning through the phone. "I know just the place."

Said place was a gay dive-bar downtown. A spattering of beautiful people of all shapes and sizes. Colored hair glittered amongst the lights that beat as if in tune with the pulsing music. We sat at the bar – Charlie with a Vodka Tonic, and me with a frozen Margarita.

"So tell me," I said. "Why did you feel the need to exclaim *'you whore!'* earlier? You were so loud that one of my books fell off the shelf."

He shook his head, took a drink.

"Sacha ghosted me," he said. "My heart is broken."

"I thought they were only DFT," I said. "They

weren't interested in anything serious. You weren't, either.”

“*Fuck me*,” he muttered, the ice in his glass clinking as he swirled his drink with a straw. “Yeah. That's what I thought. For them and for me. But we went on a few dates, you know. Nothing extravagant, but you know, Italian eateries with the checkered tablecloth. Actual candles. They liked bread as much as I did. And yeah, the sex was great, but I thought there was something more. I thought we were starting to connect.”

“Maybe they just need some space,” I told him. “Give it time. Just not *too* much time. You deserve to move on to someone as equally interested. If Sacha really doesn't want to give you the time of day, let em' go. Like a bird, they say.”

“Do they say?” he mused. “I can't even think about them without my chest feeling like it's going to tighten and snap. It's worse than when Tormund lost Brienne to Jaime, Bailey.”

“Jesus,” I murmured. “I'm sorry, Charlie. That's awful. This really sucks.”

“Distract me,” he said. “Talk about yourself. I might be a fucking gargoyle right now, but I still want to know why the major meltdown earlier. Sorry if I'm only up for giving shit advice tonight, but I'll try. I'm already buzzed.”

We were lightweights. Only one drink in, but we ordered another.

“I've been guilty of ghosting, too,” I confessed. “I haven't talked to Elijah in awhile. Not since after that deep-dive into his deviant fuckery. He's been so persistent, too. And I like him, Charlie. It's a real, goddamn crush situation here."

"Like David Archuleta level?" Charlie inquired, dead serious. "You were listening to *Crush* while you were mowing down those french fries, weren't you?"

Fuck.

"Yeah," I said. "It's that bad. I like him. He's attractive, he's charming. He's a Slytherin. I'm a Hufflepuff."

"Excellent finders. That must mean there's something about this guy that's worth tracking down."

"Excellent finders," I repeated. "Except when he tried to track *me* down, I ghosted him harder than Moaning Myrtle."

We took a sip of our drinks, pausing to absorb the music. It was heady, the room alit with the scent of sweat and something almost incense-like. The mix of pheromones and cologne and various perfumes. A few girls smiled at me from the far-end of the bar, their lips painted with dark lipstick. One had a shaved-head, thick curves, a full mouth. The other was thinner, waist-length hair – almost waif-like. They were so beautiful.

"I went to his house," I continued, pausing. "And there was another woman there. They had literally just fucked. It was humiliating."

"And you're sure it wasn't for a shoot?"

My stomach dropped. "Yeah. It wasn't for a shoot. And she was gorgeous, Charlie. No cellulite whatsoever, with legs like a Gazelle. I don't even know how to compete with a woman like that. With the women Elijah has fucked around with in general. Elijah hasn't even seen any of my cellulite or interesting fat deposits.”

“Lady,” Charlie leaned in. “People fuck up. Sometimes literally. Like, Elijah may have literally fucked this woman. Dick-in-vagina. But that doesn't mean he doesn't like *you*.”

“Bullshit,” I downed my drink. Ordered a shot of tequila. Downed that, too. “My mother used to make me measure myself with a measuring tape when I was a teenager. She wouldn't buy another school uniform if I outgrew it, because I was too fat, you know. I had to stay lean. Or at least average. But now that's all I've ever really felt. Fucking *average*.”

“Everyone's average,” Charlie said. “Some just have access to nicer cars or plastic surgery.”

We turned, scanning the scene. It was a weave of dancing bodies, incandescent lights, and House Music. It was nothing I'd ever seen before.

If we're being honest, it was the first non-work related party I'd ever gone to. I didn't party in high-school. Or college. Or ever.

“Charlie,” I said. “One more shot, then we dance.”

And so it was. One shot, then another, and then a final – mango, syrupy, sliding down our throats as if an actual medicine. A balm for the wounds.

We were wasted by the time we hit the floor. A girl approached me – doe-like eyes, a bird-like smile, and I could have kissed her. A part of me wanted to. Her hair was blue; aquamarine, long and wavy. Maybe it was a wig. I didn't fucking care. I was too fixated on the fact that her shirt was off: across her breasts read: *Melodie*.

"That's my name," she grinned. She smelled lovely, like a Parisian garden. And something else. Clove cigarette smoke, some herbal deodorant? "What's yours?"

I quickly turned to Charlie. Or at least, to where Charlie had been. He now was gone, awash at sea, lost in the waves and heaving torrent.

"Bailey," I said, my insides heavy. The booze. The French fries. "You look like a mermaid, Melodie."

"Bailey," she cooed. "Why don't you come dance with us?"

So I did. I danced with Melodie, and two stunning, proudly-declared trans boys with lashes that I brutally envied, and at the end of the song we all kissed. Sloppy, drunken, still beautiful in it's train-wreck sort-of-way. Romantic in the way you would never admit to your kids, in the later days of boxed lunches and schoolwork at the dinner table.

We went outside, into the blessedly cool air, and they smoked cigarettes. One was smoking a pipe. He took a long inhale, then offered it to me.

I wasn't thinking. Tobacco, probably. Pot, most likely.

I had no fucking idea that it was actually crack.

I took a hit. I immediately felt it: blood rush to the head, my heartbeat so loud it was like a death-knell. If this were a movie, the camera would pan in: pupils dilated, lips apart, the sudden realization that I was on train-ride of which there was no getting off. I was on this trip, whether I wanted to be or not.

The euphoria hit me like a wrecking ball to a glass wall. I'm not sure what happened to Melodie, or to the beautiful boys, but I didn't quite care. I dove back into the club, feeling entirely apart of this beautiful mesh of faces, bodies, vibrations and vibrant echoes of love and yearning and meaning and inclusivity. Everyone was valid. The scantily-clad and the full-on drag. The fake lashes and teeth glowing under the lights. I was both in and *of*.

And then, panic. I was a boat barely afloat amidst a major tidal wave. All of the many eyes were suddenly leering. The teeth belonged to demons, staring under the red lights. Beating, beating, like blood.

I yelled out, yelped. Where was Charlie? I was convinced I was having a heart attack.

I ran, a bullet through cloth, outside and nearly into the street. I pulled out my phone, my heart racing, racing, racing, and just hit send to the first number.

It was Elijah. Because of course it was. Who else could it be?

"Bailey," he was alert. He hadn't yet gone to bed. I wasn't sure what time it was, but I sensed early morning; the sun waiting patiently behind the steep rise of the many buildings. A patient woman, the sun was. Oh god, I was going to die. "Bailey, are you there?"

"I'mhavingaheartattack," I stammered. "Elijah, I'm losing touch with reality."

I started pacing, up and down the sidewalk, my insides rattling. I could have jumped out of my skin.

"I'm scared!" I yelled. It wasn't even into the phone at that point, which hung from a limp arm, barely clutched in my hand. "I'm losing touch with reality!"

"Bailey," his voice was a gentle ghost. Safe. I raised the phone to my ear, cautious. "Where are you? I'm coming to get you."

"I don't know," I said. "Bar. Downtown. There's lots of colored hair. They're playing Adam Lambert. I hate this song. 2008 was a terrible year. Also, do you ever just miss Obama?"

"Stay right where you are," he commanded. "Just – don't move, okay? Unless you're in the street. Then move. Stay away from moving vehicles. And don't talk to anyone."

His voice was safe. My heart still raced, but I could breathe. The streets were still filled with people that seemed to be moving too quickly, distorted by all of the colors. Nothing here seemed real. Not even the cracks in the sidewalk; the stray bits of grass that crept through the cracks.

What if this was how the world ended? What if that one hair-line crack in the sidewalk was actually a sign that the entire Earth was going to split in two?

And then, Charlie. His hands were on my shoulders, a sudden move that made me jolt.

"You're rigid as a fucking corpse," he said. "Bailey Mortus. Look at me. Bailey, look at me."

I looked at him. He seemed to inspect me, pausing to glance down at the way I clutched my hand, the way I tapped my foot. I was grinding my teeth.

"Bailey, did you smoke *crack*?"

"Idon'tknow. Someone offered me a pipe, I took it. They're gone. Probably forever. Charlie, I'm losing touch with reality. Help me. I don't want to die."

I slunked into him. Panic swept over me again, sudden and real and violating. It gripped me like the hands of an aggressor. I sobbed, unable to handle it. A total mess. A total fucking disaster.

"Bailey, it's okay," he murmured into my ear. "It was just a little crack, okay? You're not going to die. Let me call an Uber."

"Elijah," I said. One word. No further explanation. I wanted to run straight down the street. I realized that one of my tits was out. My bra was gone. I could feel the hair pressed against my forehead; sweat, water from the bottle that had been poured on me in the ocean dance-floor. "Elijah."

Charlie seemed perplexed, but gracefully, Elijah appeared. Charlie did his best to clean me up: tit back into my shirt, sweep the hair from my eyes.

"Is this princess yours?" he asked, amused. "She's had a rough night."

"I smoked crack," I exclaimed, not even looking at either of them. I was staring at the graffiti on the wall: *Life Is Beautiful. La Vita è Bella.* "It was just a little bit. A little crack."

Elijah guided me into his car. He played mellow music; acoustic music I didn't know. Simple strings and voices worn-down like polished wood. He held my hand, stroking it gently, reminding me to breathe.

At his house, we waited, sitting on the kitchen floor as I had so desperately insisted, until my heartbeat had slowed to a rhythm that returned me to a state of functioning human.

"You're one of the sweetest people I've ever met," I said, a whisper. "How could anyone not love you?"

"Let's get you cleaned up," I could hear the smile in his tone. I thought I'd heard him say: *no, I'm not so sweet*. Contradicting me.

I showered, borrowed a pair of boxers and a T-shirt. If this were another story, I would be sober, or maybe a bit buzzed – but in a sexy way. I'd sing a sexy-buzzed song in the bathroom as I double-checked my lipstick and made sure the tag wasn't sticking out of the back of my panties.

Then, top button undone, I'd emerge and undress and we would make ravenous love on the bed, the floor, probably everywhere. That's what happens, right?

Instead, I was in the guestroom. My head, resting on a pillow, damp from my damp hair. Elijah was kneeling next to me, stroking my forehead.

"I'm sorry I smoked crack," I said, now completely sober. Mortified. "This is the worst night of my life."

"It's okay," he cracked a grin. "It happens."

"Does it, though?"

"Hell no," he exclaimed, exacerbated. "You're a fucking loose cannon, Bailey Finch. I've never met a woman like you."

Was that a compliment? I didn't know. I couldn't, not right then. All I could do was sleep – a sound sleep, deep, awakening that morning to the warm amber sunlight, slowly pouring through the half-closed curtains. Elijah, asleep at my side, fully-clothed. He snored, as a matter of fact. Light, in kind of an adorable way.

In another story, I would have tip-toed out and made him breakfast. We would feed each other berries, whipped cream, and talk about our plans for the day.

"I've never met a man like you, Elijah Mattox," I whispered.

I found my clothes, washed, folded and resting on the floor, by the end of the bed. I picked them up, carefully crept out, and dressed in the bathroom. Sneaking out was easy enough – it was the thought of what he'd be thinking when he woke up that was hard.

I was so humiliated. I squeezed myself through the gate bars, barely fitting. Oh, those lovely curves. I heaved slightly afterwards. Even more humiliating.

I looked up, the sun bright, the clouds stretched-thin. It was quiet, with only the birds chirping. A morning we were all lucky to wake up to.

There was one person out there, I realized, that would be having the best day ever today. And this morning, this beautiful morning, would be the start of it. Maybe it was a single-mother: folding laundry in the wee-hours of the morning, wondering about what was left in the pantry that she could possibly scrounge together as breakfast for her picky children. A sullen father, stuck in commuter traffic, listening to AM radio. Sipping hot coffee and cursing the line of cars ahead of him. Would they reach their destinations before he did? Was that fair?

Perhaps a child, still sound asleep in their bed, or a grandparent, awaiting delivery from a Meals on Wheels volunteer, hopeful they might stay an extra minute to chat.

Maybe this person worked in an office, or in a warehouse. Maybe they were unemployed. Regardless, this would be the start to their very best day, even if they didn't know it yet.

But oh, not I. Not Bailey.

Bailey Finch – The loose cannon.

CHAPTER 7
For You I'll Wait

While I was away, Deborah had moved my stuff into a larger corner office, with a floor-to-ceiling window overlooking the street. That morning, it was warm and rainy. The people, scattered about, looked like paint speckles on a cement canvas. This was a thank you, Deborah had said, for the past years spent shuffling into the office, taking coffee orders and sometimes forgetting to take bathroom breaks. Nights spent over the keyboard at home, working late, the laptop screen's glow still present after I had shut my eyes.

"Also, Adam is moving into your old cubicle. Poor boy. The standing desk by the door was beginning to feel slightly degrading."

"Yeah?" I'd mumbled. I wasn't thinking about Adam, or even this nice, new office I had been relocated to. I was thinking about Elijah, wiping the damp hair from my forehead, kneeling beside the bed. I shook my head lightly. "Sorry. Distracted."

"By what, love?"

I stared blankly at the window – not through it. I wasn't looking at what existed outside.

"I smoked crack the other night. It was a bad time, Deb."

"Oh, good *grief*, Bailey. Are you alright?" she closed the office door, spinning my chair around to face her.

"What happened?"

"It's not – it wasn't terrible. I mean, I'm not condoning smoking crack, but it wasn't some fallout sort of situation. It was at a club. I wasn't thinking straight. I wasn't thinking at all, actually."

I took a small breath.

"Anyway, I ended up calling Elijah. I guess I was standing in the street, yelling that I was losing touch with reality."

"Oh, God."

"I said that a *lot*, Deb," I told her. "Like, I'm pretty sure everyone surrounding me thought I had actually lost my mind. I'm surprised that the cops weren't called."

"And Elijah – did he come and get you? Did you go to the hospital?"

"I'm not sure, should I have gone to the hospital? God, probably." I groaned. "Yeah. Took me back to his place. Bathed me, fed me, put me to bed. You know, like a fucking toddler."

"Well," Deb whistled through closed lips. "Reach out. Talk to him about it. Write about it. Find a way to weave this into your piece."

She stood, and I watched her heels click like tiny horse hooves against the freshly-waxed bamboo flooring. At the door, slightly ajar, she paused.

"If it ever gets serious," she said. "As in, if your mental health is straining, please come to me. We can scrap this project. We'll find you another one. You matter more than any piece of writing."

I smiled, blanched.

"I appreciate that, Deb. You're a dy-no-mite boss."

After Deb left, I nestled into my chair, still dazed. The small office, albeit seemingly more spacious with the large windows and bright aesthetic, was still small. I stared at my computer screen, feeling somewhat faint. Maybe it was hunger. It was probably hunger. I had only eaten half a loaf of banana bread for breakfast.

I put my head down on my desk, and everything else faded out. There was a gentle quiet, a lull. Nothing but the soft hum of the every-day business surrounding me.

That is, until a buzz broke through that soft, petal-thin barrier.

Everyone was chattering. I was swiftly jolted up by two hands suddenly grasping my shoulders. It was Mila, who wrote our Beauty editorials.

"Elijah is here," she said, half-hushed. "He wants to talk to you."

"Oh, fucking fuck," I moaned. "Never mind. That's fair. This is totally fair."

Her mouse-like eyes were wide, her lips slightly parted.

"I'll tell him that you'll meet him by the entrance."

"Tell him to meet me outside," I said. "I need air."

She scurried off. I shut my laptop, and took a quick glance at my reflection in the wall-to-ceiling glass. I looked decent, I guess. I did bother to at least put mascara on. I had some tinted lip balm in my purse. My clothes – a tea-length, ditsy-floral dress – was without any wrinkles.

Okay. I took a deep breath. *I'll fix this.*

I found him outside, turned away, scrutinizing the plaque of business names beside the entrance. The many offices with their many cubicles, and all the hundreds of people with their titles, names, coffee preferences. Sometimes the notion of all the different lives that came and went from this one place overwhelmed me. Completely neurotic.

I didn't wait for him to turn around.

"I made a complete fool of myself the other night," I said. "I'm so sorry I put you in a position like that. I'm old enough to know better."

"Hm."

He turned, slowly, and there was perhaps the smallest hint of a smile at the corner of his mouth. His eyes, however, were sad. There was a soft glisten to him – to all of him. In his black, cotton T-shirt and jeans, his sandals, his mussed-up hair. He looked just like any other normal guy.

"Do you want to go out with me?" he asked. "As in, an actual date?"

It took a second to hit me: the question. He was asking me out on a date.

"I'm not sure," I said quietly.

"Is it because we're working together?" he asked.

"No," I said simply. And that's when I decided – I wasn't going to toy around. I wasn't going to wait for the right moment – perfectly poised, written in the stars. I was just going to tell him. "It's because I'm a virgin, and you're a porn star. And I mean – it's not just *that*. You're gorgeous. Like, Zach Efron meets Ian Somerhalder. I'm plain, Elijah. Also, I gained five pounds this month. I have stretch marks on my thighs. I've tried Spin classes, squats, everything, and I'm still not hopeful that I'll ever see a thigh-gap."

He waited. His arms were crossed, his brow dipped.

"You finished?" he asked.

"No," and suddenly, it was a complete downpour. "Did you know I can eat an entire box of Kraft macaroni and cheese in one sitting? When I was in high-school, my mother would pinch my stomach pudge. Or a couple months before prom, I asked this guy out that I had the hugest crush on, and he told me that he might have considered going out with me if I weighed a little less. But just a *little* less. And then he pointed out that he could see my love-handles poking out between my shirt and jeans. I cried for hours after that. Literally hours."

He was still waiting. His look, however, had fallen. It was impossible to tell what he was thinking.

"That's not why I'm a virgin, though," I informed him. "It just hasn't happened yet. Maybe a part of it is the insecurity, yeah, I guess. But most of the men I've met are assholes. Even in my own office. Most of those guys, the nice, sweet, *mature* guys – with their degrees and half-framed glasses – are total dicks."

He stepped forward, carefully. In another story, another timeline, another life – maybe he would have kissed me. One of those long, slow-burning, passionate kisses. He would have bitten my bottom lip, and I would have moaned, and fallen against his chest.

Instead, he hugged me. An awkward, fumbled,

sincere hug.

"I'm so sorry that happened to you," he said gently. "That's terrible."

"So nothing else?" I said, technically into his chest at that point. The last part of my other-life fantasy had come true. "You don't care about my intact hymen or cellulite or that weird notion that virgins have that creepy bond-thing with the first guy they fuck? You know, the attachment thing."

"I'm not medically versed on hymens or the broader origins of virginity," he stated. "So I can't say."

"Still."

"I'm not trying to fuck you," he drew me away, his hands on my arms. "I mean, maybe someday, if you want to. But if you want to wait, that's fine, too."

"What if I wanted to wait indefinitely?"

"Sure," he said, simply. "I'll wait."

At this point, I almost meant it as a joke. A nervous, half-thought-out, clumsy joke.

"What if I wanted to wait until I was married?" I asked, pointed. "See, that's the thing about this whole waiting game. Men will wait – I mean, okay, this applies to women, too – but when it comes to waiting, people only wait for so long. They want to test-drive the car before they buy it. Sex has become so fucking commoditized. And here I am, working for a magazine that totally sells just *that*."

"So you don't agree with premarital sex?"

"That's not it," I insisted. "There's nothing wrong with it. I want everyone to live their best life, whatever that looks like. I'm just ranting. I have a lot of emotions right now."

"Evidently," he smirked. "I won't ask you if you're on your period."

"That's a fucking terrible joke," I told him. "And I am. So there you go."

We walked for awhile, just in circles, around the parking lot. I wondered briefly how many creeping eyes were peering at me from their offices above. Chirping like birds. There were no birds above us – just the hot sun, blurred against a cloudless sky, and a heat that buzzed.

I sat down on a curb, beneath the shade of a small Sycamore. Elijah remained standing, looking down at me, still appearing so sad.

"I'm so sorry about the other day," he started. "I don't have anything to say about it. I mean, I'd had about a thousand potential explanations that I'd run over in the shower and during the drive over here, but they all suck. They're shitty explanations. There's no other way to break that whole thing down other than to say exactly what it was: a quick fling with an old colleague. I was sad."

"Why were you sad?"

"I missed you," he said plainly. "I missed you, that's all."

I could tell from his face that he felt, in complete sincerity, badly. Probably for the both of us – and not himself, that is. The other woman – the colleague. He probably felt badly for her, too. For having used her.

"Yeah, that really hurt to stumble upon," I admitted. "But I was ignoring you. I get it. You owed me nothing. We were technically just co-conspirators in this big, sleazy project."

"How's it going?" he asked, sitting beside me. "The piece?"

"It's more of a short story at this point," I told him. "Definitely a longer piece. Which I'd actually like to run by you, if you want to read over it and give me any notes."

"A story, eh?" he said. "About me?"

"You and me, technically," I reminded him, and right then, I felt so nervous. Even more than I did when confessing to him that I was a virgin. "Us, I guess."

"Us," he echoed, smiling. "You know, I like the idea of that even better."

We sat in quiet for a long time. The air still buzzed, insects and dry heat, and we stared without knowledge of each other's thoughts for some time. Our eyes were forward, staring at that glassy building. Time seemed to almost stand still. I don't think either of us was certain of what the other one was waiting for.

"Sure," Elijah said suddenly, breaking through the fog. "I'll wait for you. I'll even stop the sex-on-camera business, put it on pause, figure sometime else out – focus on my other art, if that's what you really wanted. No more porn."

At that moment, even as he said it again, I believed it was a joke: "I'd wait."

"So what does this all mean?" I asked.

He paused. We walked for a bit longer, stopping to stand briefly beneath the barren branches of a small Oak. A car whizzed across the parking lot, kicking up dust.

Somewhere in the city, a heart was breaking. A phone was getting thrown across the room. There were fists clenching a pillow; a face buried in the tear-soaked fabric.

Somewhere in the city, two lovers were saying farewell.

Somewhere in the city, perhaps in the parking lot of an office building, two people were coming to a quiet understanding of one another.

Eli and I, we both felt the same way.

"I think I really like you, and I think you really like me," he said. "And I think, if you'll have me – I'd really like to date you, Bailey Finch."

CHAPTER 8
First Date: Fetish Club

So just like that: we were a thing, an item, an actual *couple*. It took a few days for me to actually realize what had transpired. I sat up in bed, awake, my phone suddenly pinging with texts like: *hi, I miss you* – and – *I'm bringing you coffee*.

And he would – he'd bring me coffee, walking straight into the office as if he were anyone else. Often his hair was messy. He wore slouchy jeans and soft T-shirts; casually gifting that simple flash of a smile when my colleagues greeted him.

Swoon. Every time. The funniest bit, to me at least, is that while Eli had been an arguable household name when it came to the Adult Industry, most of these women hadn't actually watched his work. Some had, sure, and you could tell – they sat straight-up when he was around, clearing their throats, nervously shuffling papers. For the rest, it was much more straightforward: there was a hot, charming, exceedingly polite guy loitering around our office.

A hot, charming, sweetly-sly guy – and he was *mine*.

When I told Deb that Elijah was quitting porn sooner-than-later, she threw her hands up, seemingly in a state of panic. Pressing her palms against the window glass, she didn't say anything for a solid minute.

"You're fine, love, you're fine," she said. "But this

won't effect the piece, will it? I haven't budgeted for additional articles to act as fillers. We really need something here."

I smiled. I declined to remind her that she had told me I could quit the piece if I wanted to, not so long ago. What happened to that?

"How about this?" I asked. "He's leaving for me. We're sort of dating. Well, not sort of. We are indeed dating."

She turned, eyes wide, arms limp at her sides.

"Well, that was..quick?" she didn't seem certain whether to question or congratulate me. "So you're official."

"Officially."

"And he's just going to...*leave*? What about his current contract?"

Ah, well – I hadn't considered that.

"I'm not really sure how that would work," I confessed. "But he seems confident in his decision. I didn't press him to do it." I paused briefly, searching for the words. "I'll admit, it feels a little sudden. I like him, Deb. I like him so much. I know, I know it's *super* weird, but I do. I'm completely zapped by this guy."

"And you're totally against him fucking women on-screen while he's with you."

"I'd say I'm completely against him fucking anyone else while he's with me."

"I can't say I blame you," she related. "So you have him all to yourself now."

"Well," I fumbled. "Yes."

Except, that was sort of a lie. He wasn't even fucking me. At least, not yet. I had no idea where I really stood on that matter. Earlier that week, I had walked into a sex shop, just to scan the place, and was intimidated by the various-sized dildos. And I know that makes me sound like an immature child, I get it – I'd bought my own Hitachi vibrator from Amazon, safely discreet – but what the hell was I supposed to do with a real dick? Also, they're kind of ugly. I preferred looking at Eli's face for the present moment.

"Don't worry, Deb," I told her. "You trust me, right?"

"Always, love, and again -" she stated. "Please don't do anything that feels uncomfortable. I know I sounded stressed a moment ago, but truly, we'll work around this. I'll see if Adam wants to dip his hands into writing the piece he's been rambling on about. Male thongs. Revolutionary, he says. Great package hold and apparently the sphincter stimulation is *very* pleasurable. I can squeeze it in if need be."

She hugged me, warm and lovely and smelling of sandalwood and lilac.

"We'll grab lunch later," she said. "I'll leave you to it."

So there it was. I was, in the very literal sense, the girlfriend of Elijah Mattox. Elijah Mattox, the porn star – ex porn star, now – who liked me. He really liked *me*. It blew my disquieted brain. My various woes didn't irritate him. He didn't find it weird that I preferred wearing hooded sweatshirts, even when it was warm out. And he liked to talk to me, both serious and silly.

But most conversations went a little like this:

Eli: *Will you send me a selfie?*

Me: *Depends. Is this spank bank material?*

Eli: *No. Strictly interested in seeing your beautiful face.*

I would then stare at the ceiling for perhaps a beat too long, my heart pattering, feeling suddenly like a teenager all over again. Except this time, it was in the best of ways. It felt almost like a second-chance.

Me: *You're being gross.*

He'd sent me a picture. Super grainy. His face, smiling, with stubble and that stupidly perfect smolder.

Me: *You're too hot for me.*

Eli: *OMG. No. Stop it.*

Me: *You've been in like, a million mainstream porno films. Obviously you need to be on the spectrum of conventional attractiveness for that.*

Eli: *So no photo?*

I groaned inwardly.

Me: *I look like a baked potato right now.*

Eli: *That's great. I love potatoes.*

He sent me a *Lord of the Rings* gif. Alright, alright, then. I sat up straight, smoothed out my hair, and snapped quick selfie. Hit send. My stomach immediately sunk.

Eli: *You're so pretty.*

Me: *Sometimes I get pimples in weird places.*

Eli: *When I was seventeen, I looked like a pizza.*

Me: *That's cool, I love pizza.*

And etc., etc...essentially, juvenile chit-chat. A

welcome release, really, from the every-day mash-up of sitting in front of a computer, typing out general articles about new wrinkle-zapping creams, targeted towards twenty-somethings, for Christ's sake, or whether or not vertical stripes or horizontal stripes were more flattering. All in addition to my current piece, but boring as hell. Fruitless. I honestly felt listless during these moments. The work was sometimes demoralizing, perhaps even moreso than my days of editing the magazine calendar, but it felt weird to admit that. I liked my colleagues, the benefits were great, and we were all in the same boat, really. A paycheck – needing to pay our rent, keep our stomachs full, chip away at our mountain of student loan debt. All of those many needs encased in a sparkly, floor-to-ceiling windowed cell with free snacks, decent parking, and a gym I never used. Compared to working in a call center or standing at a cash register, I considered myself privileged.

My phone buzzed, hopping along my bed-spread. It was Eli.

"Do you want to come over and watch a movie?" I asked immediately. "I haven't watched *Tangled* in forever. Have you seen it? It's my favorite movie."

"With Mandy Moore and the lizard?" he asked.

"Yeah, except it's an Iguana," I corrected. "Also, I love Disney movies, so you can write that down."

I could practically hear his smile through the phone.

"What else do you love?" he asked. I imagined him also laying back in bed, resting his head on one arm, smiling towards the ceiling fan. A soft ray of marigold light streaming through the warm, linen curtains. Soft dust flecks dancing.

"The color purple, library books where there's already a bookmarked page with the corner bent, and California rolls." I answered.

"California rolls are so pedestrian."

"Whatever, I'm boring. Do you want to hang out?"

"Always," he said, and I could hear him sit up – the exacerbated creak of his bed-frame, the even more exacerbated sigh. "Oh! Also. I want to tell you before I forget – I'm so scatterbrained lately, it's insane. I have an audition next week. It's a mainstream flick, too. Some big names behind it. I can't say too much."

I sat up in bed, too.

"Are you kidding? Eli, that's incredible! You must be so psyched. What's the movie about?"

"A guy knocks a girl up after a one-night stand. Has no idea. She eventually tells him, they try and make it work, but she dies in a car crash. The baby is saved, and he tries to raise her solo. I'm auditioning for the lead."

I was grinning madly. My heart shimmered; my feet kicked against the side of my bed playfully. I imagined him standing center-stage, the light cast across his frame, wearing plainclothes and giving an earnest smile. This – the same guy who had fucked three woman BDSM-style on a film set, his very first sexual experience captured on film. Eighteen-years-old. He was just a boy, when you consider it. I wondered what he looked like, then – I tried to. His eyes a bit softer, his frame leaner – without the sinewy, winding muscles.

Without any tattoos, his body slimmer, his mouth forming an apprehensive pout. Waiting, waiting for the Director's signal to begin.

And now, he was here. Auditioning for a main-stream film – and alongside who? I couldn't even begin to imagine the other faces and names he could soon be linked to.

I wiggled, suddenly feeling an emotion I couldn't quite identify. Uncomfortable. Anxious. Way, *way* out of my element.

I must have been quiet for a second too long, because Eli was repeating my name – cutting like a dry echo through the murky images, running like mice around my brain.

"Bailey?" his voice was slightly raspy. "What's going on?"

"I'm sorry. I'm such an astronaut," I said. "Spaced out."

"Are you okay?"

Was I? I had gone from a giddy Mary Sue to wavering, teetering on the edge of telling him that I couldn't do this. I wasn't some chill, go-with-the-flow kind of lady. This made me *so fucking* nervous – maybe because I wasn't technically over it all yet. He had told me that he would wait, but the industry wasn't something he had officially left behind. It lingered like a ghost; a veil draped across the both of us. "I was honestly imagining your first time on set – back then."

"Hm," he was then quiet, too. "What about it?"

"Was there an audition process?"

"It's mostly surface shit," he said. "They look over your photos, invite you in to talk. You strip down – naked – and they scrutinize you. It's perhaps the most dehumanizing element to it, really."

"Does size matter?"

"Yes. Tits, too. Unless you're auditioning for the role of a high-school girl, co-ed, or something. Then it doesn't matter so much."

"How young will these girls pretend to play?"

The silence between us grew; the pause thickened, uneasy with the inescapable truth.

"Technically, everyone is of-age. Eighteen-years-old. But it's not like the girl who's playing Babysitter is outwardly exclaiming that they're legal before getting railed by the Husband. Sometimes it's more insidious – outfits alluding to younger girls. There's a lot of age-play. Age-play is hugely popular."

"That is disgusting, Eli. You don't support that, do you?"

More silence. I could imagine his expression, void of emotion as he sifted through the words, mulling over his answer. A soft exhale, an uncomfortable twitch.

"No, no, I don't," he answered. "But I don't judge, either. I try not to, at least."

I guess that answer was fair.

"Eli," I started, paused, then started again – afraid of coming off as confrontational. We were so new, what did he owe me, anyway? "How are you going to just stop doing porn? Is your contract officially over? Will they sue you if you end your contract?"

"Does that worry you?"

"Jesus, Eli, of course it does," I said. "I don't want them suing you. I don't want to stir anything up for you. If you need to ride out your contract, then do it. Don't worry about me."

"It would seem strange," he said. "Fucking other women, but not fucking you."

"Does it mean anything?"

"Strictly transactional," he said quickly. "Only professional. Of course it means nothing, Bailey. It means nothing to me."

I wondered how he felt, saying that. It made me feel a certain numbness, a certain breathlessness. I swallowed, hard, and closed my eyes.

I tried to imagine the Eli I knew – the Eli from only minutes ago, really – talking about Disney movies and California rolls. LOTR gifs. The *human* behind the actor. My boyfriend.

Elijah Mattox was my boyfriend.

"I'm not sure how to do this," I said softly. "I don't know what to do. I don't want to make this decision for you."

"If clarification helps, I have four more scenes before this contract ends. They're expecting me to renew, but I have no obligations after that. And I don't give a damn, either. I'm more excited about creating something more, Bailey. Films like the one I'm auditioning for now."

"You won't miss it?"

"I'll miss aspects of it," his honesty honestly floored me. I said nothing. "These are colleagues, Bailey. I've done multiple scenes with these actresses. It's the same as leaving a desk job, emptying out your desk, clearing out your cubicle, sharing cake with overly-emotional co-workers. It's the little things you miss. There are things I'll miss too, sure, Bailey. I enjoy what I do."

Another hard swallow, another hard truth. If this were any other storyline, he'd say that he didn't give a shit about the industry. Never had, never would, and that I – the heroine – was all that ever mattered. I had led him to the light. I was enough to turn him away from the treachery and lechery of porn.

But that's not real life, is it? That's not reality. This – this sudden sharpness in my chest – the sudden urge to cry – and yet, *understanding* him. Completely understanding. That was real life.

I wiped a stray tear, quietly emotional. What was this I was feeling? I cared so much about a crush. About the subject of this grand story. I didn't love him – lord no, not yet. But God, I cared so freaking much. It was slightly exhausting.

"Finish your contract," I said, sitting up straight, suddenly bold. And I meant it. This was what I wanted. "How spaced apart are the scenes?"

"I'll be done by the end of the month," he said. "But Bailey, are you sure?"

"Yeah," I answered, soft, but not soft enough to completely give myself away. I tried to remind myself – he was still waiting for *me*. This counted. He was waiting for me, I didn't need to perform, I was a fully-fleshed person to Elijah Mattox. "I'm absolutely sure. Is it okay if I add bits to the piece?"

"It's your piece," he said. "Nothing's off the record."

"I don't think you wholly grasp what *on the record* means."

We both laughed, lightly, breaking the tension – or perhaps imagined tension, on my end. I had no idea how Eli actually felt.

"So after *this* audition," I said, conscious of my breathing. I was feeling dizzy – hungry – thinking about lunch, honestly. There was a leftover Chipotle burrito bowl in the fridge. "Do you want to come over? Or I could come over to your place."

"Does sex make you nervous?" Eli asked.

The question, unexpected, stunned me.

"Yeah," I told him. It was honest. I wasn't some sweet, virginal thing. Make no mistake. But yeah, it made me nervous. "I'm arguably unexposed to the whole thing."

"How about this, then," he proposed. "There's somewhere I would like to take you. If you'd be interested."

"Where to?" I asked.

I could picture it: the wry grin, deliciously wicked.

"A fetish club."

Here's the thing – a part of me understood that the whole relationship with Eli was possibly more than a little weird. It was quick. One moment, I was sitting on his couch, giving a simple interview – and now, we were a thing, and I was smitten, and I was watching him fuck on set and feeling sulky about it, and slightly turned on, and completely out of my depths.

I'd had crushes before. And I'll be honest, I've always been terrible about them. My feelings get the best of me. Once, in the eighth grade, I had a crush on this guy named Marvin Buttery, with the most ridiculous and honest-to-God last name of all time. I had admitted this to him during gym-class one afternoon, when the two of us had forgotten our gym clothes, so we had to sit on the sidelines of the soccer field, in the sweltering heat, and watch the other kids.

I told him I liked him, and he said that he liked me, too, and I spent the rest of the week writing his name inside all these little hearts, all over my notebook. And guess what? We never talked about it again. It went nowhere.

Cue the rest of my life. I wanted to learn, and I certainly knew better, but I was prone to getting swept up. Maybe it was Daddy issues. Likely Daddy issues.

Gross.

Either way, I was still feeling a little jumbled about things when Eli picked me up. His car smelled of those plug-in air fresheners and the last whiff of fast food. He had The Weeknd playing on his playlist, which I knew had likely been carefully crafted. I wondered, sliding into his car, if he had ever made a girl a playlist – or mixed CD, back in the day. I wondered if he had special playlists that he queued up, dependent on the mood. I

wondered if he had a certain go-to song during hookup
moments, when the lights were turned down, the air
hanging with anticipation.

I wondered what his past girlfriends had been like.
He had mentioned, briefly, dating other women – all
actresses, so they knew he was also fucking not just
them, but others, on the side. Totally fine with it. I
imagined how they must have looked: Botox-inflated
lips, breasts swelling against thin lace, long limbs and
abs defined by strict calorie-counting. No weird toenails.
My pinky toenail was weird.

I now panicked slightly, eyes widened, worrying
about that one, single recollection. I would refuse to take
my socks off during sex. Or, ever. I would be *that*
person.

Eli was watching me, side-eyed, as I shut the door
and yanked the seatbelt across my chest. He quirked a
smile, combing a hand quickly through his hair.

"I was thinking," he said, poking my shoulder. "You
should come to my shoots. You can watch them, if you'd
like. If that would make you more comfortable."

How would that possibly make me feel more
comfortable?

"That might work," I was trying to give a careful
effort in my response. "Can I write about it?"

"I told you – nothing's off the record. Write what you
want."

"I still don't think you have a full idea of what *on the
record* means."

We sped off, with him holding my hand. He brushed

a thumb across my knuckles. At a green light, he kissed
my cheek, nipped at my ear.

My heart thudded. I squeezed my legs together,
unprepared.

There were seven green lights en-route to our
destination, tucked away around the winding corners of
a tiny, Cypress-tree shrouded street in Los Angeles.

When he pulled into the parking lot, he turned to me,
and I turned to him, and I could tell that he could tell
how badly I wanted him to just kiss me. To rip through
the membrane stretched-thin between us, a transparent
barrier.

I wanted this to feel, for a moment, breezy and light.

He leaned forward, brushing a soft kiss against my
lips. His fingers traced down my jaw, resting on my
chin. Our noses touched, our eyes closed.

"Are you okay?" he asked softly. And I could tell,
right then, he truly cared. He wanted me to be okay. He
wanted this to be okay. "You seem elsewhere."

I didn't want to talk, so I brushed a finger across his
lips. He bit the tip of my finger, playfully, then kissed it.
I felt dizzy with desire, wanting him so terribly, right
then, but not like this. Not in the parking lot of some
fetish joint.

We pulled apart, his hand still atop mine. The light
through his tinted windows enveloping us in a gray
shimmer. I could still taste him – peppermint chewing
gum.

And off we went, into the night.

"This –" I stopped. "This is a sex club."

The entire span of flooring was bathed in a deep crimson; the lights, dim, casting a soft glow across the sprawling expanse. You could practically taste the flesh; the tang of sweat, of salt, in the air. Filthy. Cleansing. You could hear the muffled moans from the dark corners of the room.

There was a bar near the front. I marched over, nearly tripping over my feet despite decidedly avoiding to wear heels, and found an empty seat at the counter. Eli slid in beside me.

"Two High Balls," I told the bartender, ordering for the both of us. Eli seemed amused, raising an eyebrow, resting his elbows lightly against the counter. He was dressed in all black: a T-shirt and slacks, black belt, black leather shoes. He looked deceivingly innocent; his gaze sweetly curious as he leaned back to scan the crowd. I could see the muscles, taut, beneath the thin cotton. He had a shadow of stubble, his hair was purposefully tousled. I wore a black dress, tights, flats. I had tried to pull together my sexiest outfit, and had felt a wave of confidence when stepping out the door. But now, I felt so out of place. All of the women here were so effortlessly sexy. Leaning against the walls, some with partners, their mouths against the soft curve of a nape, their heads tilted to the side, eyes half-open. Drunk on alcohol, on the raging sex seeping from the walls of this place. It was black-paint splashes of fake-eyelashes and red lips and soft, ambient music.

When the bartender placed the drinks in front of us, I stirred mine, trying to calm my nerves. My hands, my arms, every trace of skin was bathed in the red light. Eli was bathed in red, too. It was sensuously eerie.

I took a sip. Bitter. So fucking bitter. Why did I order High Balls? I didn't even like them. I just wanted to seem sophisticated.

"High Balls are a card player's drink," Eli offered, as if knowing exactly what I was thinking. The ice clinked against the side of his glass as he took a sip. "Not that I'm complaining. I love a woman who takes initiative."

"Is that so?" I smirked. "I would have thought you were the one that preferred taking control, Mr. Mattox."

"You're adorable," he chuckled. "If that's alright for me to say. I know some women hate being called adorable, or cute. I get it."

"I don't care," I exhaled, looking up and realizing that the ceiling was actually made entirely of mirrored glass. You could see the entire area from above. That's what must have made this place feel so shimmery; celestial, almost. Or maybe it was just an out-of-body experience I was having. Maybe I was completely out of my mind. "Just don't call me sweetie, sweetie."

"What about sweetheart?"

"Sweetheart's fine. My grandfather called my grandmother sweetheart. I find it endearing."

We downed our drinks. It burned all the way down, and I visibly winced. Eli then stood, guiding me off the stool delicately by the elbow.

"I'd like to hear about your family sometime," he said. "But candidly, not right at this moment. Let me show you around."

The command in his voice settled in a weird way – had he been here before? Who was I kidding – of course he had. Sexuality, in some form or another, was his *lingua franca*. It was the bridge in which he communicated with so many around him, who in other ways he might not be able to say a word to at all.

He'd had fun with his fellow actresses in the past, sure. They were friendly. But how deep did things actually go?

Still, this had started to feel unsettling. It wasn't a negative thing, but still unsettling. I felt a strange pang of wonder and jealously and a serious case of the jitters. Who had he taken here, in the past? What was he doing here now, with me?

So I decided to just ask him.

"Eli," I said quietly, as we passed by a set of circular-shaped beds, draped with a delicate, gossamer veil, on which couples were fondling one another; sucking, kissing, straight-up fucking – completely naked – on the blankets. "Who have you brought here before?"

We watched a couple – we were welcomed voyeurs – as a man wearing a masquerade mask thrust on top of a woman, whose round breasts bounced gently. Her moans were louder than his; her red nails clawed down his back. They kissed with winding tongues. Behind them, the other couples – some hetero, but atop others were men with men – some with multiple men, some with multiple women – melded together in a singular connected moment of ecstasy.

A sign beside the Fucking Area read:
Barrier Protection Required for All Sex Acts.
Another read:
Consent Required Before Any Physical Act Whatsoever.

"Correction," he said, his eyes too on the sea of entangled limbs. "I was brought here. One of my actress friends. Actually, it was her and a friend of hers. Actress *friends*."

I could feel something burn; it felt like a sort of heartburn, actually. A sort of low-simmering fury, because I knew – my ridiculous, jealous self just *knew* – exactly what he was doing here with them. Still, I asked.

"Did you sleep with them?"

He shrugged lightly.

"Yeah," he said. "I slept with them."

"Just one of them?"

He squirmed a little; I could tell I had flipped some switch. He appeared slightly uncomfortable.

"Both," he confessed. "I slept with both of them."

"On these beds?"

"No," he said, giving me a side-glance. I looked back at him, then lowered my gaze to the floor. "It was in another room."

"Show me the room," I told him. "I'd like to see it."

Eli appeared suddenly hesitant. There was a look on his face akin to: *oh, I fucked up. This was a massive mistake.*

But he was brave, he was bold, and didn't indulge my insecurity. Perhaps he knew better than I did. He knew what I was capable of handling, and wouldn't let me play the sullen child. A part of me appreciated that, as I struggled so evidently to navigate these feelings on my own.

I needed Eli to guide me, to teach me.

"Okay," he agreed, taking my hand, our fingers interlacing. "Come with me."

"I'll say this," I said as we walked down a narrow, darkly-lit hallway. There were antique, Gothic-style sconces on the walls holding faux candles, and they flickered with a fake, dancing light against the Damask wallpaper. "This is not how I imagined our first date."

He stopped mid-step.

"I'm sorry," he said quickly, immediately face-palming. "This was a terrible idea. I'm such a fucking idiot. I've never seriously dated before. I don't know how to do this."

His sudden floundering took me by surprise. We'd been together for like, an accumulative ten seconds, and even that was generous. Yet, I was something – *someone* – he took seriously. I sifted through the meaning, carefully, picking apart the words. *I've never seriously dated before. I've never seriously dated before.*

I was the first serious girlfriend on the arm of Elijah Mattox. It floored me.

Suddenly, I was flattered. I felt a slight sense of security, a certain weight. If these past women he carried with him like a folded-up receipt, I was a carefully-written letter. I was winding script, scrawled by-hand and fountain pen.

"No," I said, certain. "I want to stay. Show me the room."

"You don't want to stay here, Bailey. I'll take you to dinner. I know tons of places around here – and no, these aren't joints I went to with other women. I've gone by myself, to be honest. God, that probably sounds pathetic, doesn't it?"

He was rambling. I stood on my tip-toes, pressed a finger once again to his lips, and silenced him.

Like before, in the car, he bit the tip of my finger playfully. God, I loved it.

"Show me the room, Eli," I said. "I want to see this place. I want to explore with you. I'm not that kind of girl. I'm not some fragile thing you need to protect. I'm just your regular ol' fashioned neurotic."

Ol' fashioned neurotic *liar*, more like. I *was* fragile. Fragile, but trying to learn. He laughed.

"Fair enough," he smirked. "Alright, come on, you."

We ran like children down the hallway, our shoes skidding on a worn rug the color of a lipstick I imagined Marilyn Monroe once wore. I felt playful and beautiful and daring. I'd done one small thing, at least – conquered jealousy, and seized a moment once shared between two others as mine, and mine alone.

When we reached the room, there was no door. Rather, the room was closed-off by a red, velvet curtain. It was draped ever so slightly to the side, signaling that the room was open.

I walked in before him, standing in the center of the room, my throat suddenly tightening. This was a dungeon – dark, grayscale, with little to no lighting. In the corner, hung on hooks, were various whips, chains, blindfolds, and a box with dress-up clothing. Slave masks, ball-gags, leather corsets.

When I turned, Eli was still standing in the entrance, seeming uncertain that he wanted to come inside.

He swallowed, hard. I watched him, his lean frame wavering like a shadow, still in disbelief that this guy was mine. It was unusual and extraordinary and enticingly deviant.

I didn't want to be that sweet virgin, that delicate little thing. But I could be – if I wanted to. It was my prerogative to be whoever I felt like being. I could do whatever I wanted – and there, in that room, that truth rang especially loud.

What do you do now, Bailey?

What will you do?

I could feel myself tremble, slightly, as I unzipped my dress, let it fall to my feet, and stepped out of it. I kept the flats on – wishing desperately that I was wearing a pair of stilettos for this moment – but that just wasn't me. I wore a simple black-padded bra – again, wishing so hard that it was lace, but the panties were lace, at least.

Eli stepped inside, carefully, closing the curtain behind him. He seemed a mix of beast and boy, with the shadows of the room falling around him.

"Bailey," he said softly. "I don't – oh, God. You're so

beautiful."

I felt so beautiful, then, too. Despite the dimples in my thighs and the slight bit of stomach pudge that I knew was all too visible while I was standing there, stark in my underwear. I felt beautiful. Unique, truly, to anything he had ever seen.

"I don't want you to fuck me," I said. "No penetration. That's a hard line. But I want you to do to me what you did to those other women in here. I want you to do to me what you've done to those women on film."

"Bailey, that's all acting," he said, his voice a near gasp. "It's not real."

"Well, then," I said. "Show me a piece of something real."

My heart was pounding – a heavy thud, a steady drum-beat.

Eli pointed to a wall on which there were a series of wrist-cuffs.

"Stand over there," he commanded. "Face the wall."

I did as I was told, stepping out of my flats first, my feet cold against the stone floor. I pressed my palms against the wall, which too was cold. I could suddenly feel the chill in this room – my skin prickled, and I shivered. Still, I kept my palms firm.

"Stand still," he commanded. He walked over, securing my wrists firmly to the wall. His movements were rough – he grabbed me by the shoulders, positioning me as he wanted me positioned. He grabbed my legs, spreading them apart. "Okay."

I could hear him take a small breath, a soft inhale: *okay*, *okay*, I heard him mumble to himself. He was second-guessing this whole thing.

I then heard it, tapping against the floor. It was a riding crop.

"Safe word," he said, his voice pitched. "The safe word is RED. Bailey, are you sure?"

I paused. I could feel my heart thrashing, crashing against my ribcage. I was in *so* far over my head, I had no idea what I was actually prepared for – physically, emotionally – any more. I just knew that I wanted whatever was about to happen.

"Yes," I whispered.

He stepped forward, and I could feel him – the heat of his body, fully clothed, which seemed to add an even greater tension to this whole dance. I was so exposed – he wasn't. He was in control. I was his plaything.

Eli's lips brushed my shoulders, brushed my neck. He planted soft kisses along the nape of my neck, gently biting my earlobe, his breath soft and sharp. He smelled of a high-end cologne; rosewood, something spiced and earthy. His breath, too, was so sweet.

I could feel his tongue run gently down my spine, so warm. The leather tongue of the riding crop, too, tracing softly up and down, almost feather-soft.

And then it hit: quick as lightening, a sudden flash. The pain was immediate – spreading up my back, to my shoulders, to my breasts.

My body clenched. I yelled out, shocked, stunned. I could feel my breath quicken, completely out of my control.

He struck me again, my shoulder, my back, my ass – over and over again. A leather kiss, burning, marking my skin with what seemed a thousand blood-red kisses.

I didn't think he'd hit me everywhere – I pictured it like the films – just my ass, nothing else. But everywhere hurt. I could feel the tears in my eyes, falling in thin streams.

But you know what? I liked it.

I heard the riding crop fall to the ground; I heard his footsteps, the sound of his shoes against the floor, the sound of his own staggered breathing.

He yanked my hair to the side, and began kissing my neck. My eyes closed in immediate response, like the other wallflower women, and it felt so damn good.

I wanted him to touch me. I wanted him to touch me everywhere. I almost wanted him to fuck me, right there, in the dungeon room of this indulgent flesh club; this bloodied, carnal gem.

His mouth was hot, so hot, against my skin. The marks from the crop still burned. As he kissed my neck, he bit down in spots, the pain causing me to yelp. He didn't stop – marking me down the nape of my neck, my throat, and finally releasing my wrists and ankles from the wall, so I could turn and face him.

There was no pause – no words between us. We kissed like primal animals, tongues dancing, hands moving everywhere. He was still clothed – his cock hard, and I could feel it. He pushed me gently against the wall, his hands suddenly gentle – as if he'd realized what he had done – and his kisses passionate, but tender.

He pulled my bottom lip gently with his teeth. He kissed my cheeks, my forehead, my mouth, so carefully. His entire body was pressed against me, and I could feel our hips move against one another, grinding.

He wanted me. I knew he wanted me. If I wasn't holding back, I bet he would have fucked me, too.

It was then I could feel it – the build up. I grabbed his waist, begging him closer, wanting to feel what I could of his cock up against me. The friction alone felt so fucking incredible.

I came suddenly, so hard, the moan loud against Eli's ear, and I could tell he knew exactly what had happened.

He pulled back, stunned, his face flushed, his smile wide. Then came the brief pause – the collection of ourselves, the re-entry into our bodies. We were once again fading back into the actual moment. I, standing there with a thousand marks on my body, so sore, wondering how the hell I would make myself presentable enough to go into the office on Monday. Would the lashes and bite-marks fade by then?

Eli, fumbling to adjust himself, still hard. I could tell he was focusing – trying to work himself down, trying to settle his own nerves.

He glanced at me, trying to bring himself into focus, and then gasped.

"Jesus, Bailey," he exclaimed. "Those marks aren't going away soon. I'm so sorry. I shouldn't have done that."

I kissed him, then – a sweet, innocent kiss. On my

tip-toes, my hands around his neck.

"I wanted it," I assured him. "I wanted this."

We laughed lightly. We dressed, then – or at least, I got dressed. We spent awhile longer there, having another drink at the bar, taking in the sights. I watched an orgy of men on one of those beds. I watched them all climax. I watched a couple – a man and woman – fuck doggy-style, hard, until he came, moaning her name. I was aroused all over again. I contemplated a trip to the bathroom. I could feel their sex, their heat, all over my body.

Later, in the late evening, we went to dinner at this local Moroccan spot with lights outside that hung like fireflies. I drank too much. I was buzzed and feeling light, and airy, and just so wonderful.

With Eli, sitting across from me, his hand in mine, his smile so lovely. This man – I couldn't get over it – this man was my boyfriend. Not just my subject anymore. My boyfriend.

"I don't want this to end," I said, half-buzzed from my second Mango Margarita. "I don't want to go home yet."

"Then let's get out of here," Eli smirked. "Shall we, into the night?"

I felt like I'd heard that line somewhere before. Either way, it worked.

We picked up a couple small boxes of wine, and drove to Venice beach. The evening had fully settled in at that point; I couldn't see the road, or the sky. I couldn't see the stars – but this was Los Angeles. We never really saw the stars here. It was all smog; the clouds, stretched like cotton, the color of bone. Smog and bone and golden sunlight.

I watched the street-lights, like lightening streams, blurred from the motion of Eli speeding down the winding roads. He had his playlist on, loud, pulsing through the speakers: he played my kind of music. The Weeknd's *Acquainted* was playing. I turned it up and rolled the window down, welcoming the highway winds.

The beach was empty, save for the litter. Crumpled fast-food burger wrappers skipped across the blue sand that was seeped in moonlight, like tumbleweeds. We found a damp spot by the water, sat down, and punctured our wine boxes with straws, like juice boxes. We watched the waves roll in quietly for a moment or two, before Eli finally spoke.

"So tell me about your family," he said. I was immediately brought back to the bar at the fetish club – I hadn't actually expected him to bring the subject up again. "I didn't forget what I said back there."

There it was. I smiled lightly.

"It's all painfully typical," I told him. "My mom wast strict, with a serious thing for body-shaming – I was a really chubby kid, and a fat teenager. I mean, it was bad enough that I felt like I needed to hide all of my pictures from Sophomore to Senior year in a box, in the basement. And I was the only child, and I guess she and my dad had issues for years conceiving, so she really put a lot of pressure on me to live up to these heavy standards."

"That must have been difficult," Eli remarked. Obviously it was, but I appreciated his indulging.

"And she was always changing where the line was drawn," I told him. "That's the thing about people that always change the boundaries. You never know where you'll overstep. Or where you'll fall behind. I always felt like a failure in my house."

I stopped, kicked off my shoes, and dug my bare feet into the sand. It was cool, welcoming.

"And my Dad couldn't stand it, either. He wasn't a horrible guy. But he was miserable, you know? My mom essentially kept his balls in a mason jar, hidden somewhere. That's not to say I approve of toxic masculinity or traditional gender roles or anything – but like, the guy had *no say in anything*. One time he took me out for ice cream on one of those lazy Sundays, when my mom was out visiting my grandmother, and when my Mom found out, she altered the portions I could have for dinner that night. I'd started counting calories when I was like, eight. Now my relationship with food wavers between meticulous calorie-counting and binging, with lapses of healthy eating. I'm working on it."

"Are your parents in a better spot now?" he asked. "Are you in a better spot with them?"

"Oh, he eventually left," I said. "Usual trope: he was fucking his secretary. He left to be with her. I haven't heard from him – sometimes I get a card on my birthday, though. He'll leave me a text. But I don't really care to call him. I don't really care to even talk to my mother, honestly, either. Though I'll have to eventually go back home to pick up the last of my boxes that I'd left behind when I first moved out."

"Why didn't you take them initially?"

"Not enough money for a U-Haul," I explained. "I had to cram what I could into my car, and had what I could afford delivered. Little stuff. Anyway, it doesn't matter. I'll go back for the rest of my shit eventually."

"You swear an awful lot."

"Yeah," I nodded. "I really do. I'm sorry. I know. It's crass. It's gross."

"It's not gross," he remarked. "Just an observation."

"What else?" I asked softly, to myself. "I'm Jewish, no living grandparents, but I have some aunts and uncles and cousins that live in Hoboken. Sometimes we get together during the holidays."

I exhaled heavily, took a sip of my wine – Riesling, because I liked mine packed with sugar – and looked up at the sky again. I squinted, trying to find the stars. No dice. Only smog. It was smeared across the black canvas like a child's handprints.

"I have to admit," I continued. "This whole thing feels weird sometimes. I mean, I like you – I *really* like you – but I'll be honest, I never expected this. Maybe if we were having sex, I'd feel a different connection. But I don't want that, not right now, and you know the whole deal – but yeah, anyway." I was fumbling. "It's just so different. I'm admittedly smitten, but also feel way, way out of your league. And I guess what feels weird to me is that you'd actually be fine with waiting things out.

You know, having sex."

He shrugged, took a sip of his wine, set the box down. I immediately started skipping through what I'd said – was it at all awkward or offensive? Who cares if he worked in the Adult Industry – he could still wait on whoever he wanted to. He didn't exist solely as a sexual being.

"Yeah, it is a little weird," he confessed. "But it's not like waiting is a promise, it's not an engagement ring. It's just an agreement. It's respect. You're worth respecting, Bailey. Despite what you might think from your past experiences."

I'm not sure what I was expecting him to say. I guess I was hoping for something romantic, something sweetly saccharine. The truth sank into me like a heavy stone, slowly drifting to the bottom of my stomach, and sitting there. That's the thing about these declarations – they aren't always some romantic, sweeping promise. He never intended to sweep me off my feet. He was just respecting me.

It didn't mean we'd stay together. It certainly didn't mean I was ever going to marry this guy – and maybe I knew that, right then, despite how absolutely nuts I was for him already. What I was feeling wasn't love – it was attraction. Lust. You know, all those feel-good hormones.

"Are you okay?" he asked, almost gentle. Like an apology, but an apology that wasn't needed.

I immediately took his hand, reassuring. That he respected me was enough. That I respected him, and who he was, and what he did – and what he needed to do, like finish out his contract – was enough.

It felt mature. I guess that was a good thing. Boring, sure. But good.

CHAPTER 9
I Guess I'll Watch My Boyfriend Fuck Another Lady

Charlie poured me another coffee, and I poured an unconscionable amount of sugar into the over-sized white ceramic mug, watching the granules fall like snow crystals.

I had my laptop open, writing frantically about what had transpired the day prior, afraid to forget it. My brain was all over the place – apart from my fingers maniacally striking the keys, all I could do was scan through Spotify, listening to each song on my weekly curated playlist for about ten seconds, and then move onto the next song.

I didn't even hear Charlie through this murky memory fog: whips and red marks on my skin; the half-moon bruises concealed by a concealer that was abhorrently expensive. Watching strange couples in their masks fuck, moan, cum. Sweet wine, sipped through a straw, and looking for the stars while sitting by the ocean. The moon hung like an ornament in the ink-streaked sky.

"That's enough sugar," Charlie poked me. "What's going on with you right now? Did you finally fuck him?"

"Nope, but I'm going to watch him fuck another woman today," I announced unintentionally loudly, to

Charlie and one other woman who was sitting on the outskirts, in a quiet corner, who sipped her latte and eyed me for a half-second. I didn't care if she was judging me. I was sort of judging myself. "I feel so weird."

"Because it's a terrible idea, and you know it," Charlie said, a towel in hand, wiping down the counter. "You don't want to go. You don't want to watch Elijah fuck some other porn star actress. It's going to fuck with your head, Bailey. You need to compartmentalize this relationship if you want to keep this thing going."

"You make me feel so childish for being the boy with Justin Bieber posters in his bedroom."

"I'm just saying," he continued. "If you have reservations about the whole thing: don't go. Nobody's making you."

It's true – nobody was. Nobody was making me. I was going solely on a voluntary basis.

And what had happened? A text convo, followed by an email asking Deb of her opinion on the whole affair, which was of course a terrible decision. She called me immediately, on a Saturday – which was big, mind you, for this woman – and told me that it would be so, *so* excellent for me to go.

But, you know, if I felt uncomfortable, ditch the whole thing. Run away. Or just don't go. Technically, it was my decision.

As for Eli, there was no pressure. Our conversation had gone down in a series of brief texts:

Eli: *I've got a shoot today. 2pm. I can text you the*

address if you want to be there.

And another, moments after.

Eli: *No pressure. I know this is weird.*

I had paused, holding my phone in my hand, feeling a mix of queasy excitement – and I guess, a sort of thrill? An unexpected chill crept over my skin, like spider legs.

Me: *I'll be there. Text the address when able.*

He texted me back almost immediately. I instantly hit up Google Maps and plugged in the address. I wanted to get a look at the exterior, if able. And there it was – a huge house. Not quite a mansion, but close enough. All I could really tell right then, though, apart from the size, was that it was painted a sort of cotton-candy, baby pink.

What was I in for?

I texted him back, moments after, the only thing I could think of.

Me: *You are wonderful.*

And he was. He was wonderful.

Eli: *I am scared.*

Except, by the time I received that last text, I had already thrown a few bills onto the counter, ignoring Charlie's not-so-subtle head shake as I dodged the sudden morning crowd, hustled across the parking lot, jumped into my car, and hit the road. Cell phone tossed on the passenger's seat. Blue-tooth, baby. I requested Siri play my favorite playlist – *Let's Hit the Road, Jack* – and Shawn Mendez' *I Know What You Did Last Summer* started streaming – albeit with a little static – through my old Hyundai Elantra's speakers.

I pulled out of the lot, squinting against the sun,

wondering how I was going to condense this whole experience down into something digestible for print. I had already clocked in at over 15,000 words. How was I going to simmer that down?

I had arrived relatively quickly – fifteen minutes – time flies, oh how true this can be. My car maneuvered awkwardly into a barely-fitting parking spot on a pot-hole-riddled side-street. I quickly scanned the houses on this street; they looked considerably normal. Not as grand as had appeared on Google Maps. The only peculiar thing about the house Eli was shooting at, was the color. It was like looking at a frosted cake. Maybe it was a deliberate thing. Maybe they wanted folks to wonder.

I silenced the playing song – Ariana Grande's *One Last Time* – and gave myself a minute to breathe. Just breathe.

I repeated this mantra to myself as I ran across the street and up the driveway, where I could already see Elijah. He was standing outside, by a pool, his arms crossed as he spoke something to someone – the director, maybe? He was still clothed in his shorts, his hair wet. Maybe he had already jumped in.

Just breathe, Bailey. Just breathe.

Stepping on set, the smell of chlorine hit me immediately. I guess it made sense, if they were filming this kind of stuff in pools, to have some strong chemicals in the water. I found myself an open spot rather away from things, beneath the shade of a planted palm tree. I hid myself behind a few camera-men, not wanting to be right out in the open while Eli was being filmed.

The actress wore a skimpy white bikini with thong bottoms. She was swimming lazy laps around the pool's shallow end when Eli skipped up to me, giving me a quick peck on the cheek.

"You came," he said, already breathless. A-ha, sir. Pun intended. I tried to smile. "I'm really glad you're here. I've missed you."

"I've missed you, too," I told him, and I did. I didn't want to hug him, though – he smelled of the pool chlorine and was drenched. His swimming shorts dripped water onto the cement flooring. "Will this be long?"

"Uh, not usually," he stated, scratching his head, looking around, thinking on it. I figured this was probably the first time he really had to think about it. "Maybe an hour. Like last time."

Had the last time lasted an actual hour? The whole thing had seemed to fly by – had I missed the director's shouting cut, requesting position revisions, requesting to repeat the same scene, the momentary lapses of laughter and perhaps groans, even, between cuts? I probably had.

I swallowed, nodding. He gave me another quick kiss – this time on the lips – and he tasted like chlorine, too.

It was show time.

I hunkered down in my spot, sitting flat down on the cement, criss-crossing my legs like we did during Circle Time in Kindergarten. I didn't really want to be looked at – I preferred to hide away as much as possible. I didn't want attention.

It didn't quite work, however. As I sat there, and as the camera-men set up, the director walked over to me, a broad smile swept across his face. He looked normal – though I'm not sure what I was expecting – just a normal, mid-thirties-looking guy, plain brown hair, plain brown eyes, wearing a flannel T-shirt and cargo shorts. He wore white Nike sneakers, like a stereotypical Dad.

"It's great to finally meet you," he said. "Eli said you'd be here. I've heard lots – all good things, all good things – though damn, we're all going to miss him around here. He's like a brother to me."

So he knew. Eli had already told him he wasn't going to continue with things after his contract ended. And this guy – I didn't even know his name – seemed to believe it was because of me.

I guess it was.

"I don't think there's any contractual fine-print stating that you two can't hang out after he leaves porn behind," I said, feeling ballsy. "He has other artistic pursuits he's hoping to focus on, anyway. It could be good for him."

He didn't seem pissed-off at my comment. Rather, his eyebrows arched, surprised. He shrugged, of all things. He didn't even have some refuting, snarky remark.

"You must really know him well, then," he said. "Well, I'm happy for him. Anyway, time to make the doughnuts. Cheers."

He was gone as quickly as he'd appeared. I didn't even have the time to think about what he'd actually said

– you must really know him well, then – before it was all starting.

The camera-men suddenly dispersed, and I was left exposed. I had full-view of the entire scene: Eli, in the pool, with the actress. They were swimming around, laughing, and then suddenly moving closer to each other – closer, closer.

They started kissing – okay, I could do this, it wasn't that bad – in a rather exaggerated way. I could see their tongues, their eyes half-way shut, their hands moving slowly to fondle one another. Eli cupped her breast, squeezed, and she moaned in response. I wondered if he was hard.

Their kisses grew deeper. Eli pulled her hair to the side, kissing her neck. My skin prickled, cold, but not freezing. There was an undeniable electrification to being the voyeur, watching his hands move, almost serpentine, across her wet body. Her wet hair, his fingers wringing, wrapping around, gripping, pulling at the strings of her bikini top, until it fell, exposing her perfect, massive breasts.

His mouth cupped around her nipple, sucking, and she moaned again, louder. When he rose, they started making out again, and I found myself moving forward, my pulse rising, unable to look away.

It was only when their lips parted, and their noses touched, that something sudden lurched inside of me – painful, like a knife-jab into the chest. It was quick, and dissipated just as quickly. But still, I felt it.

I couldn't help but bring myself into the scene – me,

there, with Eli. Kissing him. Remembering how our noses touched. The intimacy that felt so real between us.

What was this, then? I felt my face flush. What the actual fuck was this?

There was nothing I could do about it, though. Not then. I was completely ensnared – that same voice that echoes for us to drive straight into traffic, rendered me unable to look away. I was glued to the actual vision of these two. Of my boyfriend, kissing her neck again, whispering words I couldn't hear into her ear. Of the actress, rising to sit on the edge of the pool, while Eli pulled her bottoms down, revealing a perfectly-manicured pussy. Even her goddamn vagina was pretty. Her dark hair cascaded across olive-colored skin, her dark eyes flickering with expectancy.

I couldn't imagine how I must have looked, then. I was wearing khaki-colored corded pants and a baggy T-shirt that I mostly used as a pajama top. My hair was up in a loose ponytail. I had zero makeup on. I was suddenly very, very aware of myself.

Eli started eating her out, and I froze. Something stirred, ill-feeling, inside of my stomach. His tongue, his literal tongue, was up against her clit – sliding, pressing, as he moved her thighs apart, spreading her legs wider. She leaned back, exhaling soft whimpers of pleasure.

My stomach flip-flopped, but my eyes were locked.

I watched him pull his swimming shorts down, getting a good look at his perfect ass – an ass that I had never actually seen in such plain view before – and before the actress could let out one of her obviously-practiced moans, he had entered her.

One hard thrust, and she yelled out. Another, then another, and another.

No condoms. Every intimate part of his body had brushed across, had penetrated hers.

What was sacred? Was that thought totally fucked up? My thoughts, ravaging my head as Eli ravaged this strange woman's body – were screaming. *Leave, leave, just fucking leave already! You don't want to be here! You don't want to see this!*

Except I had, and I was, seeing all of it. The inescapable, genuine thrill mixed with the inescapable, gripping nausea. A part of me wanted to wank off, and another wanted to run for the hills and never look at Eli again. Ditch the whole story, beg Deborah to find me a different project, maybe just go with Adam's idea. Or even better, go back to the days where I was working on the magazine calendar and taking coffee orders. When it was mundane, and tedious, and safe.

The marks, still on my skin, burned – like Harry Potter's lightening bolt scar, and this goddamn strange lady was Voldemort. No number of showers would successfully scrub this from my memory.

My ears began ringing. I wasn't dizzy, but I felt weak.

Eli started thrusting harder, more aggressively, his pace quickening. His groans melded with her moans, inter-mingling like their bodies, their flesh pressed together. They were kissing again, fluid and hard. Biting lips, biting earlobes. Things he had done to me, too.

"You like that?" I heard him hiss. "You want me to

cum inside you, baby?"

"Oh, God, please," she whimpered. "Please cum. Please cum inside me."

He fucked her harder. My fingers coiled into fists. It was going to happen. It was going to happen.

And then it was happening. He groaned – one final thrust into her, his cum filling her, and when he pulled out, I could see it dripping down her thighs, white as cream.

He kissed her once more, their faces remaining close, and my heart sank a little.

"Cut!"

Had there been other cuts? Had they repeated scenes again? Everything had blurred together.

I glanced around for a clock, somewhere. My cell was still sitting on the passenger's seat, in my car. I had no idea what time it was. I had no idea where the hell *I* was.

Eli stayed unmoving for a moment, save for having pulled up his swimming shorts. He said something inaudible to the actress, who laughed as she dressed herself again, giving him a quick kiss on the forehead – and God, I hated whoever she was, right then. It was petty, but true.

There was something that felt so awkward about being there, all of a sudden. I didn't want him to turn around and see that there I actually was, still standing, having watched the whole thing play out. Having watched my boyfriend literally cum inside another woman. Just another day's work, right?

It was, though. Despite my rattled brain, my fears and clenched throat, it was. I just hated it. I hated how all of this felt.

Before he could spot me, same as the first time I had watched him work, I snuck out of the pool area quickly, entering from a side-door into what appeared to be an indoor deck area. There were lounge chairs and more small, potted palm trees. The room was painted in rusted reds and warm yellows. The floors were tiled, indigo-colored marble.

This wasn't enough distance. I scrambled to find other doors in this place that now felt like a labyrinth, avoiding going back outside where I could possibly be spotted, until I found the front entrance, and ran to my car. Dove into the driver's seat. Turned the engine on, started the AC, and allowed myself to actually breathe.

I glanced at my phone, finally seeing the alert. I picked it up, my breathing shaking, still feeling woozy, and glanced at the text.

Eli: *I'm scared.*

I waited, having seen those two words that should have been a comfort, to dissolve all of the strange, unfelt emotions I was suddenly feeling, that I couldn't even put a name to. I waited for the wave of relief, the sudden understanding. For the realization that what happened back there didn't matter. I was being theatrical, and overly-dramatic, and making mountains out of mole-hills, as Charlie would say.

Instead, I started crying. It wasn't a full-on heaving mess of a cry, but crying still. I tossed the phone back, placed my head against the steering wheel, and let it happen. It lasted only a few minutes, but relief came rising back, slowly, like the ocean's tide. I could breathe again.

How could this be so painful? I barely knew him, and yet my emotions – without my permission – had invested so much. A part of me had already run away with him. He held my heart in his hands like a glass ornament.

What could I do?

I met him back at his place – he wanted to take a shower, he said. The showers on set were always cold.

I waited for him in his living room, in the spot where I had first interviewed him. But for the first time, I actually looked around. Not quite snooping, but examining, sure.

I walked around the parameter, glancing at the photos on the walls – most of architecture, buildings, trees. He had none of family that I could see, none of himself with friends. There were books on the shelves, layered in dust.

I walked passed his fireplace, looking at various Blue-Ray films on the mantle. *Blazing Saddles*, *Fight Club*, *When Harry Met Sally*.

But there were others, too. Pornos. All starring Eli – and dozens of them. Arranged in alphabetical order, of all things. I picked a few up, examining them. *Whores of*

Madison County or *Allie's Anal Adventure* or *Slut Snuff.*

He was on every cover. The same face, more serious, more air-brushed – but still him. I put everything back, wishing I hadn't looked.

I waited for Eli, sitting on the couch. He returned maybe fifteen minutes later, his hair towel-dried, fully-dressed in jeans and a plain navy-blue T-shirt. He was barefoot, and smiled at me, perhaps a part of him sensing.

"Are you okay?" he asked.

Of course not. Not really. But oh, he looked so sweetly handsome. He was back – *my* Eli. The Eli I knew – except, not really.

The Eli I was getting to know.

"Yeah, I'm fine. I just got a phone-call that I needed to take," I lied. Then, a truth: "I don't want to watch the rest of your scenes. I don't think I can."

"Fair enough," he said, sitting down beside me. A part of me was hoping he would start on some grand speech about ripping up his contract, right then. Not doing another scene – telling the company to fuck themselves. But he had promised – and I had told him to keep his word. I couldn't go back on it. "Do you want something to drink?"

I wanted to deny it, but I accepted a consolatory glass of water, gulping it down slowly.

"I know this is incredibly last-minute, and I understand if you don't want to go," he started, and I could already sense what I was in for – more of what I'd seen, in some form. "But the guy you met back there?

The director – his name's Nathan, by the way – he's having a birthday party tonight. It was thrown together on a whim by some of the crew."

"Elaborate on crew?"

"Actors, actresses," he confessed. "I feel like I have to go, what with not continuing my contract. It's kind of like I'm leaving behind family, Bailey. I know it's hard as hell to understand. I can't expect you to. But I really think I should go. I just didn't want to keep you out of the loop – or keep anything from you, really. I wanted to offer you the invite, if you'd like to go."

"That sounds like it could be fun," I said, uncertain – but not quiet a lie. "Sure, I'll go."

"And one other thing – Jesus, I'm sorry. I feel like a terrible boyfriend for just throwing all this shit on you," he said. "One of my exes will be there. It was nothing serious, I swear, but there's nothing I can honestly do about it. She's big in the industry, and has done a lot of work with Nathan."

"How long ago did you guys date?"

"It was like a year ago," he said. "Maybe a little less. I honestly don't even remember it."

Should that have comforted me? Was it terrible that the fact of Eli not remembering dating someone was at all a comfort?

Yeah, it was probably terrible.

"Has she done a lot of work with you?" I inquired, pointed.

I think he was shocked that I asked. Did it actually matter? He just admitted to dating her – I knew what dating translated to.

"Yeah," he answered. "A fair amount. But again, we weren't serious. You're the first, Bailey."

A part of me felt like he was saying this just to placate me, but I knew I had to take him at his word. I needed to believe him. Even if a part of me struggled, I could see it in his eyes, too – he was rambling, anxious, conflicted. His eyes had softened; his mouth was a straight line. I needed to believe that I was his first.

I was the first. And he was mine, too.

Maybe there was still some intimacy I could find between us. Maybe it was there the whole time, and I just refused to see it. I didn't know.

"I'll go," I finally said. "It sounds like it could be fun."

CHAPTER 10
It Was Nothing Serious

Tits. Tits everywhere. Mostly huge, silicone-inflated tits, covered delicately with various shades of satin, strapless, form-fitting gowns that swept across veined-marble, their curves on full display. Blondes, brunettes, red-heads and raven-haired alike. They wore falsies and lip-gloss over their heavily-lined lips, their teeth white, as if under a glow lamp. Their contour was on-point; their makeup flawless. They were all beautiful. Sincerely, completely stunning. I was a chubby, red-cheeked cherub amongst glossy-eyed angels.

And fuck it, I felt the part.

"So many boobs," I mumbled.

Eli, who donned a full suit and Jesus, was I unprepared for that, turned to me.

"What?" he asked.

"Nothing," I said quickly. "I am woefully under-dressed."

"Nonsense," he replied. "You look beautiful."

I adjusted my dress, attempting to stifle my disbelief at his comment. Glancing around, everything appeared sort of light, airy. Everyone was so good-looking. The women outnumbered the men, by a long-shot, and mingled amongst each other as if they were all long-time friends. And they probably were. Most had probably worked together at one point or another. I scoped them out individually: the small-breasted red-head with a wide, nymph-like grin in the strapless silver gown. The mousy-haired, petite model with the mauve-stained lips and midnight-blue dress, wearing five-inch heels and thick falsies. Her milky complexion appeared familiar – I squinted slightly – and it clicked. They had worked together. She was in one of those scenes I'd watched during that evening in my apartment. The regretful deep dive into Eli's past.

Instead of letting it consume me, I asked him, point-blank, as we made our way towards the bar.

"What about her?" I asked. "The blonde with the Dorothy-red heels."

"Yes," he said.

"What about her?" I asked. "The busty gal with the long legs."

"Yes," he said.

I pointed to a few others, and was met with a prompt: yes. Yes, he'd fucked the older woman – probably mid-forties – with the auburn hair and devastatingly perfect cheekbones. Yes, he'd fucked the virgin-esque, blue-haired alternative model à la *Suicide Girls*, with the nose piercing and heavily-lined almond-shaped eyes.

"I also fucked those three," he motioned towards a group of women in a far corner, shrouded vaguely beneath the shade of a potted Eucalyptus tree, mingling together. Their laughter was like distant bells. "Gang bang."

My jaw dropped.

"You were in a gang bang scene?"

"You're actually surprised?" he appeared amused, his eyes not on me, but the bar. "I'm thinking a Whiskey Sour. Do you want a cocktail?"

"I think I'll stick with wine," I murmured, my eyes snagged on the group of ladies. "I'll take a glass of Riesling."

My chest felt tight. I couldn't help but find myself breathless, feeling out of place. Feeling as if I were being stared at as intensely as I, too, was staring.

And I couldn't lie – I was looking for Eli's ex. She was here, somewhere. Maybe she was at the bar, ordering a martini, her tilted smile infectious. Maybe she was at the hors d'oeuvre table, picking at a plate of roasted beet root or shrimp cocktail or miniature beef wellington. Silver plates were stacked with cheese, crackers, piled with plump red grapes and lush slices of pomegranate, the seeds glistening like garnet stones. I imagined this specter popping a grape into her mouth, biting down, a bit of juice running down her lip.

I was relieved when Eli returned, handing me a glass, the long stem delicate between my fingers. I could tell he sensed that I was anxious – he touched my shoulder, soft, feather-like.

"You look so beautiful, Bailey," he said. "I mean it. I've never seen a woman wear a dress like you're wearing that dress."

It worked. I blushed.

"Is there going to be another dick cake here?" I asked, jokingly. "This seems a little posh for cake and candles."

"There's a dessert table in the other room," he divulged. "I think there's a chocolate fountain. Strawberries, miniature pastries. There's a gelato bar."

"This guy must be loaded," I remarked. "I didn't think there was really much money in porn."

"There isn't," he confessed. "It's really just a choice few. This guy happens to be one of the choice few. Speaking of which, we should really find the birthday boy."

I wished we could have skipped the formalities and went straight to the dessert table. But, alas. We moved through the sea of glittering dresses and perfumed hair; parted mouths bantering, gossiping, laughing at their own inside jokes. I felt a few women glance at me, then at Eli, and lean in – a soft murmur. Words I couldn't hear. I could guess, though – *who the hell is she? She's so plain. Also, what a botched eyeliner job.*

We spotted Nathan quickly, reclining casually against a gilded statue of a woman undressed, speaking in low tones to few women who fluttered around him like moths to a lamp.

"Nathan!" Eli called. "What is all this pomp and circumstance about? You pretentious bastard."

"Piss off, Eli," Nathan laughed gregariously. "Leaving us to pursue the real Hollywood dream – I can't wait to see your Emmy award-winning TV show five years from now. We're gonna miss you around here."

"I'm sure that will hardly be the case."

"Anyway, it's my fortieth. Let me have some fun,

won't you? You know you love a pretentious party."

"Guilty." Eli grinned. "Hi, ladies."

They hugged him, he kissed their cheeks. I could feel my own grow hot as I watched them, feeling suddenly shy. They were platinum-blonde bombshells, with wide hips and tiny waists. How could I stack-up to that?

"It's so good to see you, Eli," one gave his arm a squeeze. "It's been forever. A couple years, I'd say."

"Yeah," he agreed. "I'd say at least three years. Back at the hospital shoot, right?"

"I'd rather forget about that shoot," she said quickly. "I couldn't walk straight for two days after you were done with me."

So he'd fucked her, too. Had he fucked the other two? Probably. I found myself looking at my feet, at my round toes, feeling painfully awkward and devastatingly unprofessional.

"Lila," Eli said. "This is my girlfriend, Bailey. We met when she interviewed me for an article she's working on. You've heard of *Come Magazine*, right?"

"I've been subscribed to them for *years*," she swooned, exacerbated. "You write for them? That's so cool."

She seemed genuinely interested. I wasn't sure why this was so difficult for me to digest – we weren't that different at all. Different occupations, sure. But here we were – just two women. Birthed from mothers, like the rest of the sweet-scented expanse.

"It is pretty cool," I agreed. "I really enjoy it. They're good to me."

"And you interviewed Eli?" she asked. "When will the interview be published?"

"Well, we're actually still working on the project," I told her. "It's sort of evolved from an interview into something a little lengthier. It's more of a short story at this point. I'm still on the first draft."

"I can't wait to read it," she smiled, nudged Eli, and glanced lightly over towards the other two ladies, who were obviously waiting for her. "You've got yourself a fine gal, Eli. Anyway, I'm starving. I'll catch you later?"

"Definitely," Eli said. They kissed each other softly on the cheek, gave each other another warm hug. "Take care of yourself."

We stepped away, and I felt hot. The room was packed, close. I found myself wringing my hands.

"You didn't introduce me to the other two," I said. "Was there a reason?"

"We're all colleagues," he told me. "I figured it was obvious."

"So you've fucked them, too?"

He stopped mid-step, turning to me, eyebrows raised.

"Yes, yes I have. Are you okay?" he asked. "Do you have an issue with that?"

I breathed out, hard, wondering why I had agreed to come here in the first place. I was not good at setting boundaries for myself.

"No," I said, a slight lie. "I don't have any problem with it. She's certainly radiant."

"Not as radiant as you."

"Oh, none of that," I stressed. "I'm not that kind of

woman."

More lies. Yes I was.

We agreed silently to let it go, walking towards the dessert table, blessedly covered in a spread of fruit and chocolate. I scurried over to the strawberries, piling them onto a glass dish along with mini tiramisu, eclairs, and sliced melon. Eli dipped his spoon into a large scoop of pistachio gelato, and we ate quietly, listening to the sounds of the guests and the music – light piano – as it tried to force itself through the crowds.

I decided to drop the bullshit, and enjoy myself. I bit into a strawberry, suggestively, licking my bottom lip. Eli smirked.

"You're a bad girl," he said. "You're so delightful."

"You're damn right I am," I told him. "And right now, I want another drink. Do you want something?"

"I'll have another Whiskey Sour," he said, kissing me on the forehead, tender. I felt, for the first time since walking in, of any real importance.

As I walked towards the bar, I suppose I was surprised by the fact that there weren't waves of women competing for his attention. He drifted so casually through the halls; a beautiful ghost. I suppose here, he was just another player in a greater game. It was the outside world that viewed him as something else – otherworldly, almost.

I ordered another Riesling, taking a moment to breathe. Was there even air conditioning in here? I sipped my drink slowly, leaning against the bar, just people watching. A few men – actors, I assumed, came and went, nodding at me. One asked: "Are you with Eli?" and when I said yes, they just nodded, a subtle approval. A few minutes later, an actress approached the bar and smiled at me, waiting on the bartender, a few crumpled bills in her hand.

"I haven't seen you around before," she said. "Are you friends with Nathan?"

"Sort of. Actually, no, not really," I said, suddenly acutely aware of myself. "I'm with Eli."

"Oh!" she exclaimed. "You're his date?"

"Girlfriend," I said, confident. "It's a brand new thing, though. We're only recently official."

"Ah," she said, appearing surprised. "I wouldn't have guessed, admittedly. But that's so wonderful."

I wasn't sure if I should be offended or understanding. Like, yeah, I get it, I'm kind of pudgy. I wouldn't have guessed me, either.

How self-deprecating had I become?

The bartender approached her, and she ordered a Mojito with muddled mint. She stirred her drink with her straw, took a small sip.

"I'll see you around," she said, giving a small wave, her heels clicking like cloven hooves. "What's your name?"

"Jane," I lied. Plain Jane.

I felt a mix of relief and nausea after she had left. My skin was prickled with this unknown sort of anxiety – I knew I wasn't out of place here, but at the same time, I was. I totally fucking was. Were there any other non-actresses here? Any other non-actors? I wasn't sure. It sure as hell didn't look like it, but what did I know? I wasn't exactly out in the crowds, shaking hands with people. One of those people, somewhere, being Eli's ex-girlfriend, who I still hadn't forgotten about.

I was completely over-reacting. In my purse, I took out a pad and a pen, jotting this down. It was petty, but it was useful. I had to be honest if I wanted this story to be any good. I didn't want to paint myself to be anything other than the honest-to-god imperfect, redundantly insecure mess that I was.

I suddenly felt faint, the room feeling a little too warm. I turned to the bartender, busy wiping down the counter, and he smiled at me.

"Is there a bathroom around here, somewhere away from the crowds?"

"Upstairs," he said. "By the swan fountain."

Swan fountain? Of *course* there was a swan fountain.

I navigated my way through the party, locating the staircase, the same veined marble as the floors. I tried imagine myself as a princess, or some Victorian mistress, transplanted into another story, far away from this. I was Beauty, and Eli was the Beast.

The swan fountain was as glorious as I imagined it; the crystal water gently sputtering into the basin below. It was perhaps the most relaxing moment of the evening, sitting down at the edge of that fountain, listening to the water sounds. I wondered if Eli was looking for me – wondering where I had disappeared to with his Whiskey Sour. Wondering if maybe I had left.

I took my phone out, checking for a text. Nothing.

Whatever, it was fine.

I stood and meandered into the bathroom, which was plastered in a crimson wallpaper, a red deeper than blood. The mirror was huge; the frame created to look like heavy, golden vines. There was even a deep, clawed bathtub.

I searched the room for a paper towel dispenser. Of course there wasn't one. Instead, there were towels neatly folded beside the sink. I wet one, dabbing my face, sighing heavily.

I looked at my reflection in the mirror. You know, I really did look beautiful. My eyeliner, albeit a little lopsided, was a fine attempt. My smokey-eye was overall on-point. I wasn't wearing any foundation, so my skin had a natural glisten to it. No highlighter, no contour. I had worn a little lipstick, but that had since faded to a light-cherry stain on my lips. My cheeks had a natural rouge from the pressing warmth.

I sighed again, standing in the silence, savoring it. Until that is, I realized the room wasn't actually silent at all.

Turning, I heard a small, almost mewing sound. A lost kitten. It was coming from the bathtub.

"Hello?" I asked, uncomfortable. Uncertain. "Are you alright?"

I cautiously drew the curtain back, revealing a crumpled little thing with soft, strawberry-blond waves and dripping mascara. She was sobbing, her knees to her chest, her bare arms wrapped around bare legs. Her purple gown was pulled up to her waist. It had the

lightest shimmer to it; the same color as the shadow on
her eyelids.

I wasn't sure what to do, so I walked over to the sink,
selected another cloth, and dampened it with some warm
water. I handed it to her, saying nothing, wondering if I
should say something or leave.

"Do you need some help?" I decided to ask. "I can
get someone."

"I'm fine," she finally said, more of a choke. "I'm just
a mess right now. It's been a rough night."

I sat down beside the tub, deciding that I was perhaps
welcome to share this space with her. Deciding to dare
it, at the very least. She didn't seem fit to be alone.

"Do you want some water?" I asked her. "Or
something else to drink? I could go to the bar and get
you something."

"I'm fine," she repeated. "It's pathetic, really. My ex
has a new girlfriend, and she's somewhere around here, I
guess. I haven't seen her. Anyway, what's your name?"

"Bailey," I selected, careful. "What's yours?"

"Cora," she said, wiping her cheeks with the cloth.
We met eyes, then. Hers were a deep crystal-blue pool. I
imagined schools of exotic fish, coral wreathes, warm
sunbaths. "I don't think I've seen you around before."

"I'm not an actress," I told her. "Just a date."

"Yeah," she mumbled, her eyes rolling away,
suddenly distant again. "Coming here was a mistake. It's
never a good idea to show up in the same places as an
ex."

"Can't say I've been there," I confessed. "What's his

name?"

"Eli," she said. "Eli Mattox. He's around here with his new girlfriend. I thought I was over him – it's been months – but nope. I'm sure I sound like a train-wreck."

I suddenly found myself without a single word to grasp onto. This was Eli's ex. Eli's beautiful, beach-haired ex-girlfriend. And I was his new girlfriend – the cause of this woman's pain. The Ice Queen. If I touched her, maybe her heart would freeze. Maybe that would be a blessing to her, if only for the moment.

"That must be terrible," was all I could manage to say. "I'm so sorry."

"It's fine, really," she sniffled. "It's fine. Do you even know Eli? Not that there's anyone here that *doesn't* know him."

Should I tell her the truth? Leave it out in the open, transparent. I was his girlfriend. I'm the reason you're in this bathtub right now, smelling of a too-sweet floral perfume and dark ale, sobbing.

I stood, shifting on my feet. Our eyes met again, and here it was. The moment.

"I don't really know him," I lied. "I've seen him around, but that's about it. I'm so sorry you're going through this. Are you sure you don't want me to get you something to drink?"

"No," she said flatly. "I'll clean myself up and pull myself together. I'll be out there in a bit."

Fair enough. I grabbed my purse and quietly left, closing the door behind me, sucking in a deep breath. Finding a moment of solace on the edge of the swan fountain.

This was something else, that's certain.

When I found Eli, he was already holding another drink, chatting it up with a man in a finely-tailored suit, dark eyes, dark complexion. He smiled brightly at me before shaking Eli's hand and disappearing into the crowd.

Eli approached me, looking worried.

"Where'd you go?" he asked. "You disappeared on me."

"Bathroom," I said quickly. "There was a line. Anyway, one more drink, I think."

I had another glass of wine, careful to not lose myself. I didn't want to get drunk. I didn't even want to get buzzed. I just wanted to lighten this feeling of awkwardness, which I knew would prove to be useless. A pencil's eraser against ball-point ink. It was only going to bleed and run.

Should I tell Eli what had happened? What if I met Cora again? What if we came face-to-face here, in this place, yet again. With me on Eli's arm. What if that ended in disaster? I had no idea what she was capable of. Maybe she would flip out, lunge at me, pull my hair. Full-on cat fight.

Or maybe it would just hurt. It would hurt her to see me with Eli. It would hurt her that I lied.

I sighed softly, finishing my glass, setting it down on the counter.

"I really need to get home," I told Eli. "I've got work to do."

"Wait," he said. "Just dance with me. One dance."

Through the speakers, Ed Sheeran and Justin Bieber's *I Don't Care* was playing, which was a song that felt almost laughable, but oh-so catchy. Eli stepped back, swaying his hips, which *was* laughable. I couldn't keep a straight face.

"Fine," I said. "One dance."

He took me by the hand and led me to the dance-floor, and together we moved and weaved through the crowd, his hands on my body, our mouths brushing close at moments. I could feel the warmth of his hand on my lower back, my hair damp with sweat. But we laughed. I don't know the last time I actually laughed as hard as I did when he dipped me, out of the blue, and I almost entirely fell.

"I'm not exactly light," I told him. "I'm a whole lot of woman, baby."

"You're the most gorgeous woman in here," he swore. He twirled me again. "I've never danced before. Did you know that? This is a another first."

Was it, really? Another laugh escaped me. I was smiling like a fool.

And there it was – out of the corner of my eye – I saw her. Cora. Watching us.

I couldn't quite read her expression – pained, unquestionably. Questionable, certainly.

I'm sure she was wondering who I was. Not just a girl she'd met in the bathroom. Not just some nobody.

Our eyes met. My lips parted as if to say something, but I said nothing. Before I couldn't even take in a breath, Eli dipped me again, and when he lifted me, she was gone.

Eli's face was flush, sweet, jovial. He smiled at me, brushing the damp hair from my forehead, and kissed my cheek.

"Are you okay?" he asked. "You look like you've seen a banshee."

I smiled weakly.

"I wish I could stay here with you all night," I told him. "But I really think it's time for me to get home now. I have a long night of work ahead of me."

The rest of the weekend seemed to come and go. Eli took me to dinner at a small, hole-in-the-wall Thai place, and we ate potstickers and drank Long Island Iced Tea and spent the evenings in a happy, mellow buzz. We tried again to find stars amongst the smog; he pointed out hazy constellations. He kissed me in his car to a soundtrack that I'd aptly named *Sad White Boy Music*. We held hands quietly, sitting in the warm, humid air, listening to the cicadas, perched on the hood of his car.

"Are you nervous about that audition coming up?" I asked him. "It's a pretty big deal."

"Yeah," he said, his eyes focused on the far away buildings. We were in the canyon, on the edge of a cliff. The many windows from the houses below seemed to blur, like candles. "A little nervous, I guess. But I guess it's just a different version of what I've done before."

"I mean, yeah," I told him. "But this is real acting. Not, you know, just fucking on camera."

He shifted, his mouth falling into a slack line.

"It's still acting," he said, and I tried to pretend that his tone hadn't dropped. A little cold. It prodded my heart like the tip of a dull blade. "We're still actors. We still provide something. It's not nothing, Bailey."

My legs were warm against the hood of his car; the metal heating my skin. We were drinking .99 cent cans of Arizona iced green tea and eating snack cakes from the local convenience store. My hair was tangled from the whipping wind; I tried to neaten it. I tucked the front strands precariously behind my ears, quieted, uncertain how to respond.

"You're right. Shit. I'm sorry, Eli," I told him. "I guess I do have some mixed feelings about everything. My self-esteem is just garbage. I don't know how to feel sexy when I've never really been a sexual being. And here I am – surrounded by the hottest ladies in Los Angeles. It makes me feel awkward. Younger than I actually am, I guess. I used to think that I was the perfect fit to interview you. And I'm not saying that I *wasn't* – but I guess I just wasn't prepared for you, Eli."

He turned to me, smiling. He took my hand, running his thumb over my knuckles. He raised it to his lips, kissing the back of my hand gently. I could feel my skin prickle. My heart danced.

"We're not so different," he said. "You might have not been prepared for me. But I wasn't prepared for you either, Bailey Finch."

CHAPTER 11
I Want You To Want Me

I was halfway finished picking through a bowl of pesto penne with grilled chicken when my mother called. I wasn't at all hungry – Deb had hired a contractor to paint my office walls a fresh shade of glaring Fuchsia, and I could feel my temples pulsing from the lingering smell of wet primer.

I was on an upswing, however, since Eli had texted me with news that the audition had gone well, as far as he could tell. I'd asked him if they had invited him for callbacks or anything. No, he'd said. But they didn't outright reject him. The director, a Ukrainian-born woman with blue hair and a wiry grin, told him that she appreciated his work, and oh, was he as *dreamy* in-person. And to top it off, he'd managed to line up two other auditions – albeit for a pharmaceutical and airline credit card commercial – that he was amped about.

So feeling good, I picked up.

"Bailey," she started immediately. I could hear clanging in the background – pots, pans. "Wait – just a moment – I'm in need of help with the kitchen sink this afternoon and apparently the plumber I've hired has an inclination for being entirely *destructive.* Could you please be careful? That dishware is older than you!"

I held the phone away from my ear. I could spot Deb through my door – leaning over Adam's desk, her

cleavage highlighted so that her chest seemed to
glimmer slightly. She wore a plum-colored lipstick and
soft blush that made her fair skin look velvety and
sumptuous. Her hair was tousled, light waves, falling
just over her shoulders.

"Mom," I said, clearing my throat, slightly zoned-out.
"What's up? I don't have much time left on my lunch
break."

It took a solid minute before she returned, having put
the phone down. I could hear her – fuzzy, distant, ever-
demanding – but the noise had stopped.

"Bailey," she repeated once returned. "I'm sorry
about that. There was a situation."

"I hope the dishware was salvaged."

"Fortunately, yes," she said. "In any case, I just
wanted to reach out to you about the boxes that I still
have in the attic. They've stacked up quite a bit, and I'm
in need of clearing some space in the house for some old
items in your Aunt Paula's storage unit. She can't afford
the monthly payments, apparently, so they want her stuff
out – though why she can't afford a $40 monthly
payment despite her apparent cigarette budget is beyond
me."

"Judging, mother," I told her. "No judging. Just help
Aunt Paula. I'll come by to collect my stuff soon."

Where would I put it, was the question. I had zero
space in the apartment. Charlie had a storage unit of his
own – maybe he had some square-footage he was
willing to share – but also, maybe it was about time that
I looked through the boxes and decided what I could

keep and get rid of. When was the last time I'd even opened those boxes, anyway? Two years?

I just have a thing about getting rid of stuff, I guess. A sentimental streak. Or maybe I'm just a pack rat.

"How is work?" Mom asked, cutting through my brain-fog, and the question itself almost stunned me. Short and yet, her tone was earnest. "I've been thinking about you. I know it can be grueling work. I hope they aren't working you too hard."

"Well, it's not like I'm in manual labor or some service-sector gig," I told her. I was appreciative of the sentiment, of course, but I didn't feel like I deserved the same acknowledgement as someone who woke up at the crack of dawn to serve coffee to the truckers and store-managers, slugging through the morning to make it to their next destination. All said, mine was a cushy gig. "But it means a lot that you've been thinking of me. It's not been hard work. I've been working on a pretty immersive assignment lately -" I picked up a pen, twirled it around between my fingers. "- I've been enjoying it. It's been fun, actually."

"Oh? What's the assignment?"

How was I to even begin explaining this to my mother?

"It started as an interview – he's an actor – was, no, *is* – and has transformed into more of me following him around and writing about his life. We're friends."

"Are you in the piece, too?"

"Yeah," I swallowed. I was suddenly finished talking about this. "I'll be sure to keep you in the loop. I'll send you a copy of the magazine once it's published. How does that sound?"

I spotted Deb at the door, looking in another direction, laughing. She had a long neck – graceful, swan-like. I wondered briefly what she might have looked like when she was a teenager. Did she have pimples, or was she ever pudgy? Did she have stretch-marks? Did she ever need to stuff her bra? I was lopsided, and until I finally gave into it, stuffed one side of my bra with extra padding for over a three years. Talk about a self-imposed hell.

"So, the boxes -"

"I'll have to look at my calendar, but I'd say in the next few weeks I can make it up there and grab the boxes."

"Maybe you could stay for the weekend?"

"I'm not sure. Maybe one night."

Deb knocked on the door. Therein, my escape was laid out.

"I'll cook a brisket for you and clean the duvet. Just let me know, Bailey. I love you."

I smiled, motioning for Deb to come inside.

"I love you too, Ma."

An audible sigh escaped me as soon as I hung up. Deb flounced in, pulling her hair back into a low ponytail, as if her hair were a display only meant for certain eyes. She took a seat by the window in the small, red, faux-leather chair, crossing her legs. She stretched her arms, smirking at me, impish.

"So that party, huh?"

"Yeah," I muttered. "Talk about a mind-fuck. His ex-girlfriend seeing us together, too. It gave me the heebie-jeebies. But I'm probably over-thinking it. I'm sure she doesn't actually care."

"Jilted exes can care a *lot*."

"I'm not sure if she was jilted, per se," I divulged. "I just don't think Eli and she wanted the same thing."

"Thus, jilted. I'm sure at least she sees it that way," she stole a glance outside the window, brow furrowed. "But things are certainly getting juicy."

"Ugh, I hate that word."

"Delicious, then."

"Better. That's a better word," I swiveled in my chair, pensive. "But this is getting long, Deb. Pages. I'm not sure what I'll need to cut or keep."

"Keep it all," she said quickly. "It's all worth keeping. You never know what might prove useful."

"As in?"

Deb's shrugged lightly, deviously.

"I've shown what you've written so far to a few friends – from higher places, so to speak. If this goes well, who knows, maybe we could look at broadening the project. A book, perhaps."

"With *me*, as the author?"

"Who else? Of course, let's see how this goes. And I certainly would be commanding a small percentage for the referral." She winked, and I couldn't tell if she was joking or not. "I'm kidding. Alright. Back to work, then."

She sauntered out, the smell of her powdery, vanilla

perfume lingering after the door had closed.

I sighed again. It felt these days like I was always sighing. Reset sighs, I liked to call them. Not because I was mad, or sad, or even bored. Just...I'm not even sure what I'd call it.

I glanced at my phone. It was 1:40pm. Only a few more hours left here, and I was free.

I nestled the tip of my pen in my mouth, chewing lightly, imaging myself something seductive. I wondered what Eli was doing. Probably watching TV. Maybe organizing his Blu-Ray collection. Maybe having lunch somewhere downtown, signing the occasional autograph for a guy that just *really* appreciated his work. I pictured them as being tall – lanky, chin-length hair, unwashed and potentially wearing a Fedora. Tip tip, m'lady. Yikes. Or conversely, a more alternative-style chick, much more traditionally hotter and cooler than I, that's into the BDSM scene. Maybe she tries to buy him a drink.

Suddenly, Adam popped in, his mousy, ash-brown hair disheveled, his face flushed, which gave me pause. Had he been fucking around? Moreover, I hated that he had interrupted my thought spiral. I might have hated those, too, but it was still a moment for indulgence.

"What's up, Adam?"

"Deb told me to tell you that there's a thing going on tonight, at the Roosevelt Hotel. We're all meeting up at the Library Bar at eight o'clock."

"*We* as in?"

"All of us?" he squinted a little, as if he'd managed to confuse himself. "Deb decided that she wanted an impromptu social gathering. And for you to bring Eli."

"Why? So he could be obnoxiously poked and prodded at like the gorgeous piece of prime rib that he is?"

"Probably."

I groaned. Did I even have anything to wear to this event? The dress that I'd worn to Nathan's birthday party was dirty, and I had no time for dry cleaning. The dress I'd wore to Eli's first house party had managed a grease-stain that no amount of scrubbing could wash clean. Maybe I'd hit up a store on the way home, find something quickly and not too insanely expensive.

"I'll see if I can make it," I told him. "Could you possibly grab me a Vitamin Water?"

He perked up. "Which kind?"

"I don't know. The pink one."

He returned moments later with a chilled bottle and bag of salsa-flavored Sun Chips. God love him.

"Adam," I said. "You might get a lot of shit around here, but you're invaluable, and I hope you know that."

He gave me an endearing wink, and closed the door. I grabbed my phone, texting Eli immediately.

Me: *Plans tonight: you, me, Library Bar.*

It took a few minutes for him to get back.

Eli: *What's the event?*

Me: *Forced social for work. I also figured we could celebrate your successful audition?*

Eli: *Only if you wear something leggy.*

I smirked.

Me: *Don't push it, Mattox.*

I wasn't exactly planning on attempting to seduce Eli. Which I'll just say, right off the bat, failed miserably. I mean, horribly. It was horrible.

Still, it hadn't been something I put much thought into, until I was standing on one of those raised platforms in a little boutique shop dress, thumbing a price-tag that was completely cringe-worthy, and looking at myself in the mirror.

And damn, was I feeling myself. I loved my body in this dress. I didn't care that my arms weren't toned, or shoulders defined, or that I had zero thigh-gap to be located. If Eli wanted a thigh-gap, he could stick his head between my legs. I mean – when the time came for that.

I loved my stomach, the soft rolls, my thick hips. And I didn't care that my slightly-asymmetrical breasts might have been measurably small by comparison of those women at Nathan's party – this dress made my curves look killer. It was sleek, black, and I felt like I belonged in some movie about a badass woman fighting NYC's seedy underbelly nightlife.

It was a leggy dress, too. I smiled, lips pursed, at the mirror. Tucked my hair behind my ear. Took a few deep breaths.

“I love it,” I exhaled, doing a little wiggle. “I'll take it.”

Was the dress worth $350? Hell no. I could scrutinize

the stitching in spots, the quality of fabric – but I couldn't put a price on how it made me feel. Fucking *fine as hell.*

And I guess that's when it hit me: sitting in my car, with the windows rolled down, The Weeknd and Lana Del Rey's *Lust for Life* flowing like ribbons through the air. I kept the song playing while I showered, shaved, applied my makeup. Repeat. Repeat. Repeat. I felt warm, intoxicated, hot-blooded.

I wanted to fuck Elijah Mattox.

We met up at the entrance, around a crowd of cars, the valet scanning us with a timid curiosity. The place was moody, dark; dimly-lit with plush couches and music that seemed to bloom from the walls. There was a group of maybe twelve of us, and we settled in with a fluidity that made it feel as if we'd all been there many times before – in reality, I'd never even heard of this place. I was candidly expecting there to be books, but there were none to be found.

Eli was dressed in all black – black jeans, black V-neck, his hair combed back. When he arrived it was still damp, which told me he must have taken a shower. He smelled clean. Crisp, like Irish Spring body wash and something minty. I wanted to kiss him immediately, but thought better of it. Not in front of everyone, at least.

When he saw me, his mouth gaped open. It was the perfect reaction – you look like a codfish, I imagined saying, but didn't.

I simply strolled past him. I wanted him to check me out. Inside, he bought the entire group a round of drinks and we sipped quietly for awhile, listening to the music, leaning back against the comfortable couches. Deb, who drank only martinis, bit the olive from her toothpick and chewed delicately, swallowing as if swallowing a pebble. I could feel her eying us, dying, *so* curious. The rest of them, too. Come to think of it, it seemed as if I was privy to the most interesting piece that *Come Magazine* was releasing in awhile. Talk about lucky.

"So Eli," Deb started. "You look fantastic."

"Thanks," he said evenly. "It's a new T-shirt."

The group laughed, and Eli smirked. I felt him loop an arm around me, and was suddenly warm. It was a nice feeling – noticed, protected. Would it be wrong to say that I liked feeling as if I belonged to him, at least right then?

"Do you want to tell them about your audition?" I asked him. "Is it okay that I'm talking about it? Shit, I should have asked beforehand."

"It's fine," he remained cool. "I had an audition for a film this afternoon. It went well. I've lined up others, and I suppose I'll see how it goes. I'm trying not to dwell too much on it."

He explained the plot and his potential role. They nodded, Deb leaning forward, genuinely intrigued.

"Anyway, here's hoping for a callback," he said, sipping his Old Fashioned. I felt his fingers graze my shoulder, a thumb running in circles, softly. It felt so nice. "It's a pleasure to actually meet the group of fine folks that Bailey here works with. She's incredibly passionate about this project."

"She's a good egg," Deb smiled. "We're lucky to have her. I'm lucky to have all of you," she quickly added, careful to acknowledge the other staff. "I just thought I'd get us all together for a few drinks and some chit-chat."

Eli smirked.

"Do you all have burning questions you'd like to ask me, Deb? Well, I'm here for it."

I think the team was taken aback. They glanced at one another, then at Deb, as if for direction. Seemingly, they weren't that interested in talking about their projects – I tried interjecting. Beau was working on a piece about beard oil. Moira was working on an advertisement for eyebrow-bleaching cream. Josef was playing the editorial eye on Moira's piece, Adam was covering male thongs, and so forth. Michele had the most interesting piece, in my opinion: *Vibrators Through the Decades*.

"Indeed," I muttered, tilting back my drink. I offered to buy Eli another Old Fashioned as a means to briefly escape to the bar, and he let me, bless him.

When I returned, I nestled back in with Eli, cozying up. He draped his arm across me again, giving me a quick peck on the cheek after I handed him his drink. This seemed to stir the group – oh, you two are adorable – Bailey Finch, *oh la la*!

"I was telling them about the pool-side shoot," he explained. "They were curious."

"Ah," I said. "Well I had floor-side seats to that

event. Stirring, it was. Riveting performance, Eli."

It was all I could do: try and be dry, quirky. I didn't want to hear about the pool shoot again. I didn't even want to think about it, really. I was so over it. I didn't want to think about him coming inside some other woman whose name I don't even remember.

But at least that chapter had closed, right?

"What was it like watching the guy you're dating fuck another woman?" Moira asked pointedly. "Wait. Fuck. I'm sorry, that's a personal question."

Suddenly, I was confronted: not only with the question of my feelings on the whole experience, but Eli and myself. How did it feel to watch *my* man fuck this thong-wearing woman in a pool? How did it feel to see his cum dripping from inside of her?

I didn't feel like beating this around with a stick, and I wanted to be playful, so I just turned to him.

"Do you like me, Eli?" Here I was, Bailey Finch, taking initiative, being cutesy. "Because I like you an awful lot. I'd say that explains how I feel. I watched him fuck, I watched him finish, and he comes home with me."

Well, not yet – but maybe tonight was the night.

"Exactly," he told them. "Bailey is my favorite person. I'm not sure I've met someone with such a sincere authenticity as Miss Finch."

What a gracious way to describe my bouts of insecurity. Everyone seemed to soften and swoon. Deb's smile was lingering, her eyes misty.

"I'm not even in the middle of this, and I'm in love,"

she said. "That, or it's been one too many Apple-tinis."

I took to having a third Mai Tai. By the end of it, I was sufficiently tipsy, but not drunk. Buzzed, but cognizant – able to make out the defined shapes and colors of the room around me. Nothing was blurred. All of the sounds and voices were clear and all responses, all things considered, articulate. No slurring here. This was deliberate. I wanted to feel good, but I didn't want to get hammered. Not tonight.

When Deb broke away to grab a water at the bar, I turned to Eli.

"I want to be alone with you."

His eyebrows rose, surprised. Could he not believe such a notion? I might have been wearing the dress for me, but the lace panties and demi-cup bra with extra padding were all for him.

I leaned forward, whispering in his ear close enough so that my lips brushed against him. I wanted him to feel me.

"I want you," I whispered.

He drew away, eyes wide, and then leaned in, kissing the corner of my mouth.

"I'm hard already," he murmured, his breath warm. Around us, at least, the attention had seemed to fade. Deb remained at the bar, chatting it up with another patron, with Adam lingering nearby. The rest of the crew were caught up in their own conversations. There was our moment to escape. "Do you want to get a room?"

"Yes," I said.

It wasn't until we got into the hotel room that things went awry. I might have been calculative about how much I'd been drinking, but it seemed like Eli had not. He wavered back and forth as he walked.

"I'm not *that* drunk," he swore. "I promise I'm not going to get sick. I wouldn't embarrass myself like that."

A sudden flashback forced itself back into my head – me, at Eli's, getting sick in his bathroom after my dalliance at the club. God, what a hot mess.

In the room, he seated himself on the edge of the bed. I undressed slowly in front of him, and he watched with heavy eyes – hungry, intoxicated, his hands clutching the bedspread. I could see his erection through the soft fabric of his jeans. There was a glisten of sweat across his forehead. I could hear his breath – sharp and soft.

I stayed in my panties and bra, letting him soak me in. Then, like a slinking kitten, I stepped over to him, crawled onto his lap, and kissed him.

I could feel him, hard against me. The friction was again incredible. He kissed my mouth, bit my bottom lip, ran his tongue down the length of my neck. God, I knew he wanted it so badly.

But my hands were in his hair, and my arms were around his neck, when he gazed at me – how, how would I describe it? Dotingly. Like I was the most precious thing on Earth. Like I was a ruby in his hands.

"Not like this," he said finally. "You wanted to wait."

"Not now I don't," I told him, in earnest. "I want to

do it."

His hands fell from my hair slowly, falling next to him. He began drawing small circles on the bedspread, his eyes lowered. I suddenly felt chilly, exposed.

"We've both been drinking. You are so beautiful," he looked at me again, and any chill I was feeling melted. "I want to really know you, Bailey. Before we go any farther. If we do it now, there's no going back. I care about that. I care about you."

I care about you. The words hung like crystals. I was worth waiting for. I was precious.

"You're so sweet," I said softly. "I care about you, too, Eli."

We ended up ordering pizza, and after, dessert and coffee via room service. I took a hot shower. We flipped through the TV channels. We made shadow puppets on the walls. I told him about my mother, and he told me a little more about his.

"She was a very sad, forlorn woman. Generational trauma," he explained steadily. I could see a sadness in his eyes. "But she did her best."

"I've got to visit mine in a couple weeks to get some boxes," I told him. "Is it bad that I'm dreading it? I feel terrible complaining about my mother."

"My past does not negate your experiences," he said plainly. And then, a stunner: "Can I come with you? I mean, depending on how auditions go. I'd love to go with you."

I sat up, holding my mug of coffee. I took a long, slow sip.

"You really want to meet my mother and eat brisket and sit in my musty old house while she talks about how fat I was in high-school? Plus, Jersey's a plane-ride away."

"It sounds like a grand time," he said. "I'll buy the tickets."

Charlie was sitting criss-cross on my bedroom floor, toying with one of my threadbare sweaters. He pulled lightly at the string, and I watched the sweater slowly unravel, wordless. I was going to turn it into a dish rag, anyway.

"So let me get this straight – you tried to fuck him, but then ended up inviting him to meet your mother?" Charlie asked. "I've met your mother. He's never met your mother. Your mother is..."

"Yeah. I know," I agreed, only half paying attention. I had been working since getting home. My laptop was balanced on my legs. I'd clocked in another 20,000 words. This had far surpassed even something meant for a magazine at this point – and there was still more to be said. I had no idea how to dilute this, to whittle it down. I'd spent all Sunday morning writing about the party – strategically omitting Cora, of course – and sitting in the canyon, drinking cheap canned tea, my tongue coated in sickly-sweet sugar. "I don't know. It's kind of nice though, isn't it? We're an item. I'm his girlfriend. Eventually, you meet the parents."

"You best hope your mother doesn't find out about his – ahem, previous occupation," Charlie remarked. "He was in porn. Technically, still is. The internet is forever. I doubt Mama Finch would love that."

"That doesn't matter," I insisted. "Besides, we're not fucking. If somehow she ends up privy to that information, she'll be pleased enough. Not like we haven't done *anything*. He *did* whip me in the dungeon room of a sex club. That's something, right?"

"Well damn," Charlie exclaimed.

"It's just different," I told him. "We do things differently. That's not a bad thing."

"Do you think you'll want to go further with him? I know, I know. The whole waiting-until-marriage thing. But do you want him to want you, Bailey?"

I threw myself back on the bed, glancing at the remaining glow stars on the ceiling. Most had fallen down, tossed in the trash bin. There were maybe a handful left – not glowing. Muted. Not really even stars at all.

"Yeah, I do." I confessed. Because I did. I wanted him to want me. I wanted to evoke the same desire that those women at the party could – *hello, Nurse*. I wanted to feel like Jessica Rabbit. I wanted to bring men to their knees. "More than I could tell you."

"Anyway," Charlie picked up a crumpled Target receipt, glanced at the line items, tossed it away. "I wish someone would write an article about how much of a slut I was in a past life."

"*Do you*?" I groaned, tossing a pillow at his head.

After Charlie went to bed, I did something stupid. Morbid curiosity sat like a little demon, whispering on my shoulder. Should I look at YouTube videos of how they make Sour Patch Kids, or Eli fucking on camera?

I opened my laptop, went to Pornhub, and looked up Eli. I found all the clips of he and Cora – known as Jasmine Fox – and watched them, one by one. Cora, kneeling in front of Eli, with his hands around her throat; tears in her eyes, choking, moaning. Eli, fucking her, her long hair draped across an ivory bedspread, feathered. I could see everything up-close: his dick sliding in and out of her, her fervent moans, the cum shooting everywhere. Every scene was a version of the same: was she licking-up milk from a cat bowl, or being whipped with a riding crop, or strung up on some wall with chains, her long limbs trembling? She seemed to cum just by his touching her – sucking her heavy, round breasts, whipping her clit, fucking her doggy-style while she screamed that she wanted it *harder*.

When I closed my laptop, I could still hear her begging.

I could still picture the curve of her body under Eli's hands.

I could still picture them kissing; their tongues sliding together, fluid, snake-like.

I could still picture Cora, sitting in the bathtub, a wreck. Or the look in her eyes when she saw me dancing with Eli, as if I had caused her deliberate pain. Worse than what I'd just witnessed on-screen. How did that not leave scars?

I sat in the dark, quietly, for some time, forced to reckon with the fact that these clips, the films, everything – and not just the stuff featuring Cora – would be around forever. Eli was leaving the Adult Industry behind, but he would still linger here, always. A relic of the permanent black-hole that was the internet.

I had just a couple weeks left before the project deadline, too. I had to figure this out. I had to come up with some kind of ending – fictional, factual – one way or another.

I went to bed, and tried to remember Eli and I, in the hotel room, making shadow puppets, his laughter light and childish. Instead, I dreamt of myself on that same bed as Cora, slick with cum and sweat.

CHAPTER 12
Won't You Be Mine?

There wasn't much time for me to ruminate on my stupid decision to do another Pornhub deep-dive, since Eli arrived at my door that morning, breakfast burritos in tow, unfathomably merry for someone who was about to spend a weekend in New Jersey.

Charlie answered the door, clad in boxers and holding a cereal box.

"Very fuckable airport attire," he remarked, stepping aside. Eli gave him a small grin.

"I prefer to dress comfortable when I travel," he said. He was wearing sweatpants, a hoodie, and a pair of stylish Nike basketball sneakers. He took a second to glance around the apartment – the kitchen, with dishes still sitting in the sink. Charlie's collection of Amazon packages that he'd yet to open, balanced on the dining room table, along with a stack of neglected mail. The floors needed to be vacuumed. Really, the place was a sty.

I was sitting on the living room couch, wrapped in a blanket. I hadn't showered yet, my hair was a mess, and I was still in my pajamas. I hadn't even brushed my teeth.

"You're early," I told him. "You've caught me having my usual moment where I decide that I don't want to go visit my mother."

"It's important that we go," Eli said. He sounded so reasonable. It was almost annoying. "You'll be happy when it's over, at least."

"I still need to shower," I looked at the foil-wrapped burrito extended in his hand. "I'm not hungry. I can't eat right now."

I opted not to mention that I was still feeling slightly nauseated from last night. Jitters, he'd chalk it up to. In any case, Charlie swooped in and grabbed the burrito, unwrapping it with an excited zeal. He flopped down on the couch beside me, took a big bite, and grabbed the remote.

"No more *Gilmore Girls*," he snapped. "Take a shower, hippie. Don't leave the man waiting. Eli, you and I can watch *Practical Jokers*."

Eli sat down on the couch, albeit a little hesitantly. He looked at me with a sort of worried expression, which I suppose was understandable. I looked a mess.

I sucked in a deep breath, finally standing.

"I'll be quick," I said. I thought for a second about giving him a peck on the cheek, but remembering that I still had morning breath, quickly decided against it. Instead, I left Eli alone with Charlie, which in itself was anxiety-inducing.

In the shower, I tried to shake off the gross feeling that was still kicking around like a bad cold. *It doesn't matter, it doesn't matter, it doesn't matter*, I repeated to myself. That is all over, now. And it didn't matter to begin with, because it was only his job. He was just doing his job. It never meant anything.

And so what if maybe it did? We're all entitled to a past. Who was I to be such an insecure brat? Who was I to indulge these feelings when when I *knowingly* went digging, once again, into his online portfolio?

It was my own damn fault.

I followed Eli's lead and decided to dress comfy: a loose-fitting henley, sweats, and a pair of sneakers. I tied my hair into a loose bun. I opted against makeup, thinking I might try and nap on the plane, but made sure to bring a stick of eyeliner, mascara and some lip balm with me in my purse.

When I finally grabbed my bag and threw on my sunglasses, Eli was standing by the front door. He was ready to go. I wondered what Charlie must have said to him, but I couldn't spot Charlie in the living room. His seat was empty.

"He's not here," Eli said, as if reading my mind. "Got called into work, I guess."

"Maybe I should go into work today instead of the airport," I mused. "Or we could literally do anything else."

"You need your stuff," he said. "And I really want to meet your mother."

"Nobody's met my mother before," I informed him. "Literally. Except the few choice friends I had in high-school that met her at the odd-event. I've never even had a sleepover. Oh, and Charlie met her once, but that was a fluke."

"I'll be the first non-fluke visitor, then," he smiled, almost politely.

He was so patient. I was being such a kid about this whole thing. But that's a part of baggage, isn't it? It starts when we're kids – before that, even – and I guess sometimes, that little girl remains frozen, somewhere untouchable.

Reclined in our first-class seats, which Eli informed me was absolutely necessary, he asked:

"Does your Mom know about me?"

"In what way?" I asked him. "Does she know that you're coming? Yes. Does she know that you're my boyfriend? Also yes."

There was a delightful thrill in imagining the look on my mother's face when she saw Eli: yes I, Bailey Finch, could score a guy that looked like Elijah Mattox. He liked me just as I was, pudge and all.

"Does she know about the magazine piece?"

"Yeah," I said, and she did. I left out the more explicit details, of course. "She knows you're an actor. Very impressed."

"Is she aware that I was in porn?"

"No," I said flatly. "I left that bit out."

Eli became quiet for a moment. I panicked silently. Oh, God. I fucked up.

"I get it," he said after a second had passed. "It's kind of weird to just blurt out on the phone. Besides, she should get to know me first."

"You're not mad?" I asked, almost desperately. "I've got a thing against lies of omission. I don't know – I feel weird. I'd understand if you're pissed."

"Not pissed," he insisted. "I really do get it, Bailey.

Besides, none of that matters. Even if we don't tell her anything, I'm sure she'll read your piece eventually. By that time, I'd like to think she wouldn't have a problem with it. I'm just a guy who's infatuated with her daughter."

"You'd be surprised what my mother has problems with," I muttered quietly.

Eli leaned in, kissing my forehead. He took my hand in his, which felt small and childlike underneath his large palm and long, delicate fingers. He held my hand tenderly.

"Hey, Bailey?" he whispered. "I really like you."

I softened against him. It felt so good to at least have one, single wall start to come down. I breathed a small sigh of relief.

"I really like you, too."

I couldn't remember the last time I'd visited Jersey. I mean, I guess it's one of those places where you leave and aren't exactly supposed to even *want* to return. In college, whenever I told someone I was from Jersey, it didn't even illicit a verbal response – at most, a wince, or a cringe, or an *oh – well, I love New York!*

My Mom was a yuppie, though. North Caldwell, New Jersey, where all the upper-class white folks lived. There was about as much diversity as a box of glazed doughnuts. But it was home.

Suddenly, driving past the clusters of faded-brick

buildings, resting my forehead against the cab window, I was filled with an untouchable sense of nostalgia. Even if my childhood and tween and teenage years were arguably shitty. Even if I hated mostly everyone I went to high-school with. Even if I didn't much like myself – coming home had me feeling weirdly peaceful.

"I've never been to Jersey," said Eli, watching the buildings and cars pass. The sky overhead was heavy and gray, tempting rain. "Just New York."

"Did you go often?"

"Not really."

"Business or pleasure?"

"Both," he answered plainly, turning to me. I smiled.

"I just want you to know," I decided to inform him in advance. "My house is big. My mother has an even bigger personality."

"Duly noted."

"I put *myself* through college," I said, finding myself clenching my teeth. "Just so you know."

"Now I know," he said. "Anything else?"

I paused, blinking.

"I think you have a vague idea on the rest," I muttered. "The house is going to be impeccably clean. Don't put your feet up on the sofa. Also, the sofa is covered in plastic. Be prepared for that."

"So she's *that* kind of Mom?" Eli laughed. "At least I know what I'm walking into."

"Hardly," I snorted. "She won just about all the material crap in the divorce. She likes to keep it crystallized. Maybe it's satisfying."

The rest of the drive was quiet. I needed coffee. Scratch that – I needed a strong drink.

I felt Eli nudge me.

"You okay?" he asked.

"Mixed bag," I answered. "I think I missed the East Coast. I'm just not so sure I've actually missed my mother."

Mom was waiting for us at the door. The house, scrubbed-clean, smelled a mix of lemon wood polish and faintly of bleach and something akin to coffee. Thank God.

"Bailey!" she exclaimed, throwing her arms around me. "God, I've missed you."

"I've missed you too, Mom," I found myself automatically saying. "How are the ladies over at the country club?"

"Lorie made Matzah Ball Soup for the occasion," she said. "And I'm making a roast. Roast and potatoes. I hope your boyfriend likes red meat. He sure looks like it. Strong build."

Eli was standing behind me, peeking arguably sheepishly over my shoulder. It was the first time I'd seen him look this nervous around another person.

"Mrs. Finch," Eli extended his hand. "It's so fantastic to meet you. I've heard so many great things. I'm Eli."

"Eli. Strong name, too. You can call me Barbara – Mrs. Finch has long-retired."

Was she trying to flirt with him? Oh, God.

We went inside and settled in for coffee and shortbread cookies. My mother made the coffee intentionally strong, and no amount of cream seemed to lighten it. It was thick to swallow. We listened to her talk about the latest issues with the kitchen sink, and the new wallpaper in the downstairs guest bathroom, and how her hairstylist was back off the wagon after catching her husband in bed with their son's babysitter. She only paused to take the roast and potatoes out of the fridge and pop it into the preheated oven.

Still, she didn't miss a beat when she closed the door, turned to me, and finally asked:

"So, how long have you two been dating?"

"A few weeks, ma'am," Eli said. *Ma'am*? "But I'll say, you've raised one hell of a daughter. Brilliant writer. Great head on her shoulders. You should be proud."

"I am," my mother said, but the words came out dryly. Was the crack in her voice emotion, or was it the air in the room? "Bailey has always been the light of my life."

"Is that why you used to measure my waistline once a week in middle school?" I almost asked. Instead, I just said: "I'm actually pretty tired from the flight. Are the boxes in my room? I might go take a nap before dinner and have a look around. Eli, would you help me?"

Eli stood, still holding his coffee cup.

"I'll take this with me, if that's okay?" he turned to my mother. I wonder if he thought asking to take a cup of coffee would translate into *I'm going to be drinking this* versus *I'm going to try and sleep with your daughter*.

She nodded curtly, but her eyes were soft. She looked almost disappointed.

"I'll let you know when dinner's ready."

Eli and I stood at the threshold of my childhood bedroom, which hadn't changed much since I'd left for college. The walls were painted periwinkle, barren except for a few watercolor paintings that were of my mother's choosing. She didn't like the idea of posters or anything that might leave a garish mark in the wall – tape residue, a push-pin hole, stripped paint. My bedspread was a white lace quilt that reminded me of a paper doily. The curtains on the single window were yellow and blue calico flowers. On the bureau were bottles of nail-polish, a box of Q-Tips, an old hair-brush and a few aged bottles of Bath and Body Works body-spray – old-school Cucumber & Melon, Cherry Blossom. I couldn't spritz them now; the smell made me sick.

Eli stepped in, walking around the boxes that were stacked on the floor. My mother must have brought them down from the attic. He touched the bedspread, the curtains, ran his finger along the bureau. His breath was quiet, his gaze scattered.

"So this was your room?" he asked. "It's bright."

"It's boring."

"What's wrong with boring?" he asked. "I've got nothing wrong with boring. You're looking at someone who might have fucked on camera, but I've spent many a day off watching television re-runs and eating Tasty Cakes, thank you very much."

"Boring is...dull."

Eli shrugged.

"Maybe you'd feel differently if you saw the trailer I grew up in," he said. "Boring is safe."

Boring is safe. Safe. Was I safe here, in this boring room with the painfully-blotchy watercolors on the wall or curtains that smelled of gathered dust? I could weave my fingers through the bedspread, like a spider-web. Those covers kept me warm at night. I never technically was cold, or starved, albeit always hungry from one fad diet or another. I had a flash-vision of Atkins protein shakes and grilled chicken breast, no salt. A side of steamed carrots or broccoli. Or bowls of bran cereal or Special K while my mother made Belgian waffles for my father. Sometimes, I would steal a bite. Sometimes, I would even run my finger along the side of the mixing bowl while it was sitting in the sink, to get a taste of the batter. Maybe there was a straggler blueberry. Those were lucky mornings.

I caught my reflection in the bureau mirror, and saw that awkward teenager with a muffin-top, trying to suck in my gut, acne creeping up my nose like a bad rash. My forehead was so oily. It still was.

"I'm not sure," I said quietly. "I'm not sure if I was always safe here, either."

Eli set his coffee down on the floor and began examining the boxes. They were all carefully-labeled: CLOTHES, PICTURES, MISC. There were a lot of clothes – I'd fluctuated sizes frequently growing up. I'm not even sure why she bothered keeping all of the clothes boxed-up.

I knelt down and opened the box of pictures, rummaging through the frames carefully. They were mostly school photos, a few photo albums. I selected one of the albums and slid it out, thudding heavily onto my lap.

Eli scooted closer to me, and together we flipped through the pictures. Many of them were of me as a child – riding a pony on my 10th birthday, making pizza with my father, making latkes with my mother. Grinning cheekily on the front steps, holding up a paper sign that read: *my first day of 3rd grade!*

"You were adorable," Eli said. "I don't have many photos from when I was a kid. Or any pictures of my folks together, actually. That's your Dad?"

"Yeah," I said quietly. "That's my Dad."

"You're a good mix of both your parents," he observed. "I look just like my mother."

He smiled, sullen, flipping a page. He skimmed his finger along a photo of me with braces, sitting at the kitchen table, the candles of a birthday cake lit and waiting for another year's wish.

"Tell me more about your mother," I suggested, wanting to change the conversation, to instead learn more about him.

"She was very loving," he said. "A very sad woman, though. She dealt with a lot of unmanaged depression. I think it got worse after I was born. Postpartum domino-effect. Plus, my Dad wasn't in the picture, so she did it all on her own. Doing odd-jobs. She worked at a cleaning company for awhile before going into customer service, but was always getting sick, because of the mold. She had bad lungs."

He paused, flipped another page, sighed gently.

"She loved me, though," he said. "She was very warm. Always happy to make a cup of hot chocolate or let me change to channel to something I wanted to watch. A lot of needs, though. When she eventually needed to stop working – failing kidneys – I picked up a lot of the slack. It was never one of those things that was intended to go on for as long as it did, it just...it just did, I guess. I've never resented her for it. Besides, I like my life. I'm glad that I was able to take care of her."

We were both quiet for a moment. He closed the album, setting it back in the box. We peeled open the box of misc. items. Mostly loose pieces of old school-work, notebooks with old History or English notes, some bad poetry, a few sketchbooks of doodles. There was a trophy for Model UN and another participatory trophy for Field Day, back in Middle School.

"She killed herself," he said suddenly. "That's how she died."

I went cold. "Eli."

"It's okay," he insisted. "It's okay. I can talk about it. It's important to talk about it."

I didn't need to ask him what happened. He told me.

"It was while I was in LA, so I didn't find her or anything," he made a point to note. "I got a call from the hospital. If there's one regret I have, it's that I was a little drunk. I'd been partying. The doctor on the line kept trying to tell me that she'd passed. She'd hung herself, likely because her kidneys were on their last leg. Maybe because I wasn't there with her – sending money isn't a replacement for companionship. But it just wasn't setting in."

"Jesus."

He nodded. "Eventually I sobered up, and it hit me. She didn't have a funeral. I went back home, had her cremated, and scattered her ashes over the ocean. She loved taking me to the beach when I was little. I never talked about it much, after. I suppose I've never seen the point, outside of therapy."

"Still. You must miss her."

Eli gave a struggled swallow. "Yeah. I think about her often. She would have loved you."

I tossed the things back into the MISC. box. I didn't bother opening the clothing box. I didn't see the point. Instead, I kicked it hard, only to watch it slide an inch. It was a heavy box.

What was it that I was feeling? Sad. So sad. Sad for Eli, sad for myself. Sad for my mother, even, maybe. It was hard to even think straight. All I could feel was a dull pain in my ribcage; every pulse of my heart hurt.

I started crying. At first, quietly, just a little. Then, full-on sobs. Eli quickly swept me into his arms, kissing the top of my head, pulling out all stops to comfort me.

"Bailey," he whispered. "What's wrong?"

"I'm just so *sad*," I wept. "I should hate my mother. But I don't. Even though I hated myself for years, for no reason at all. I felt ugly, and unhealthy, and unworthy, and unprotected. My mother couldn't control my father, so she tried to control me. I became a project, not a person. I should *hate* her. But I don't. I'm sorry for her. And I'm sorry for you, and your mother, and your difficult life, and that you needed to grow up in a trailer and worry about an alligator living in the pond in your backyard. That's hardly safe."

He kissed my forehead again, whispering my name into my hair. Soft, warm, safe. He felt so safe. I sank into him like a warm bath.

"And I did something so *stupid*," I decided to confess. "I went online and watched a ton of video clips of you, and your ex-girlfriend. I met your ex-girlfriend. She was at the party, drunk, in a bathtub. She was a total mess. I think she misses you. But that's not the point – the point is, I watched all these video clips, and I honestly almost threw up. I felt so sick. It's been so hard for me to wrap my head around some of the content you've made. I know, I *know* that's not *you*. It's not who you are. But I can't shake the images, Eli. I can't get them out of my head."

He stroked my hair, my face, so tenderly. For awhile, he said nothing. He simply held me to his chest, his arms wrapped around me, rocking me, as if I were a child. And I suppose I felt like one, right then.

"Bailey," he said. "Bailey?"

He tilted my chin to face him. I could feel the tear-marks running down my cheeks, in small rivers.

"I love you, Bailey Finch," he said. "All of that other stuff? It doesn't matter. It just doesn't matter. Only you matter, Bailey. You matter. And I love you – you're the only woman I've ever loved."

I could feel my heart wrench. My face was burning, I knew my cheeks were probably stained, reddened, my lips chapped. I could barely straighten out my breathing.

So instead, I buried my face against his chest.

"I love you too, Eli," I said against the warm cloth of his T-shirt. "I love you."

I was able to clean myself up in time for dinner, and was, to my surprise, ravenous. I could smell the garlic, peppercorn, the roast fresh from the oven. The house was warm with baked bread. The soup was on the dining room table. There was a heaping pile of salad in a large wooden serving bowl.

"It all smells incredible," Eli said, nodding to my mother. "I don't know the last time I've had a home-cooked meal."

"What do you eat?" my Mom asked, seating herself. We began the ritualistic Passing of the Plates: potatoes, roast, salad, soup, until all were served. "You don't cook for yourself?"

"Mostly take-out these days," he confessed. "Though

I'd hate to actually add up my restaurant bills in a given month. I'm sure I'd be able to buy a second house with the money I'd save from buying groceries and cooking at home."

"Bailey tells me you're an actor," she continued. "And that she's profiling you for this project she's been working on. What sort of films have you worked in?"

I cut into my roast, took a big bite, chewed carefully. I almost choked. There was no water on the table.

"It's mostly independent work," he was choosing his words carefully. "More streaming-based than silver-screen. Although I did have a very promising few auditions recently. Fingers-crossed."

"Streaming?" my mother asked. "So, Netflix? Hulu?"

He scratched the back of his head, cutting me a side-glance. I decided then to just gun for it.

"More like Pornhub," I told her. "Or a multitude of other adult streaming websites."

My mother literally dropped her fork.

"Pornography?" she asked quietly. She glanced back and forth between us. She hadn't even touched her food.

Eli took a bite of his potatoes, chewing like a mouse. I stepped in for him.

"*Filthy Doctors, Slutty Patients: vol. 5, Don't Fuck My Heart, Fuck My Face*, or *Cum Dungeon*." I cleared my throat, adding: "I'm actually really proud of him. He's worked really hard. Incredibly hard. And now, anyway, that's all behind him, Mom."

"Bailey, I -" she started.

"Wait," I insisted. "He loves me, Mom. And I love

him. And I'm supportive of him – all sides of him, all pieces of him. I just want to be honest with you. I want you to love him, too. Because that matters to me."

Because you matter to me, is what I was actually saying. Because she did. Despite the dysfunction. Despite everything, everything she had done. Despite the anger I still felt, that still crept up, that still kept me up at night. She was my mother. She was a human being that had also suffered immense loss, and pain, and had massively screwed-up.

But I still loved her.

"Bailey," my mother said quietly. "I think that's wonderful."

"You do?" I asked, surprised.

"I do," she said. "Eli, are you serious about Bailey?"

"More serious than I've been about anything else in my life," he swore. "She's an incredible woman."

"She is," my mother agreed. "Not that I've made it easy for her. I have a lot of regrets."

I have a lot of regrets. It was then, hearing those words, that I didn't even need an apology. Somehow, that was enough. Any of the residual, caked-on resentment or bitterness I had felt was slowly melting away. She regretted how she raised me.

In the background, Eli's phone went off. He let the first round go to voicemail. When it went off a second time, he stood, embarrassed.

"Just a moment," he said, sliding out of the room and into the kitchen. He'd left his phone on the kitchen counter.

I looked across the dining room table at my mother. She looked older; worn, tired. It's not like anything had been magically resolved – maybe it was time for a therapist, for the both of us. But it felt so crazy, right then, that just a few simple words could be so healing. Validation. It's not for nothing.

She reached over and took my head.

"I'm happy for you," she said. "I really am."

"I love you, Mom," I said. "I love you so much."

Eli returned, phone-in-hand.

"I got the part," he stammered. He was white as a sheet. "Not the commercials, either. *The* part. The big movie. But...they need me back in LA in the morning. Formalities. I'm so sorry."

"No!" I jumped up, hugging him. "That's amazing. We'll figure it out. We'll just have to head back. Mom, I'm sorry our visit has been cut short."

She was glossy-eyed, elated. It was written all over her face.

"Please. Don't worry, this is important. I'm so proud of you, Bailey," she said. "Maybe next time, I'll visit you."

"I'd like that," I told her. And I really meant it.

I opted to toss the box of Misc. items. There was nothing I wanted to save. I opted to donate the box of clothing to the local Goodwill. As for the photos, Eli insisted these were important to hold onto. He crammed them all into his luggage, every single album, and together we sat on the suitcase cover just to zip it closed.

We took a red-eye back to LA. Eli ended up falling asleep shortly after take-off, so I took the time to write.

What I didn't expect was to finish the project.

I mean, here was as good a spot as any to conclude things. I met a porn star, we fell in love, and he moved away from porn into this big-budget film, towards a new passion. It wasn't just about the potential fame – he was living his truth, unapologetically.

I sent the final draft over to Deb before the plane landed. She replied almost instantly.

Amazing, she said. *I'll have Adam take a copy-edit pass. We should be set to launch it online by end-of-week. Print details to come later.*

Closing my laptop, I sighed, looking out the window. It was dark – no stars, no clouds – just the glare of the dimmed overhead lights. I was tired and wired all at once.

I rested my head against Eli's shoulder, and tried to sleep.

CHAPTER 13
The Big Release

To say that the *Come* piece release was massive would be the understatement of the decade. To say that this should have been one of the proudest moments of my budding young career would also be the understatement of the decade. To say that the morning of the article's release, I should have been happy – no, *elated*, was the understatement of the century.

Instead, it was a complete shit-show. Perhaps my biggest fuck-up, however, was that I didn't see it coming. Not just that, even – it was as if I had been *begging* the universe to completely fucking implode these past several months with wide, open arms.

It started with a dick cake. It started with spilled coffee and awkward banter and a mysterious, dreamy-looking man with cool-guy sunglasses and nice hair. It started with me making a complete nerd of myself. And instead of going ahead and buying a new dress, getting a blow-out, and buying the same replica of the dick cake that Eli had ordered when we first met, I should have just read the goddamn story.

Let's start there.

Charlie woke me up at 10:13am, after I'd managed to oversleep.

"Bailey!" he hissed. "Bailey! Wake up!"

I groaned, rolled over, peeked at my alarm. *Oh,*

fucking fuck.

"I slept in!" I lamented, my words muffled into my pillow. "I've gotta call Deb. She might think I'm dead. Maybe she thinks I panicked the night before the big release and drank myself into a coma."

"You're way too self-involved to drink yourself into a coma," he grinned. He was sitting on the edge of my bed, dressed for work. His apron was draped across his lap like a napkin. "Anyway, you've got a missed call. Maybe it's her."

He picked my phone up off the floor and tossed it onto the bed, promptly stepping out. I grabbed the phone, half-expecting it to be Deb, but also half-expecting it to be Eli.

It was Deb, though. She'd left a voicemail.

Darling, the voicemail said. *We've hit over 30,000 views and counting! Can you even believe it? If you haven't left for work yet, take the day off, but stop by the office this afternoon, around four o'clock. Bring friends!*

My heart thumped. You'd think that would be sufficient enticement to click on one of the dozen emails that my colleagues had sent me, all including the link to the piece. The paper magazine had even hit the shelves – and I received a hundred texts of the glossy cover, featuring Eli front-and-center, his eyes smoldering. The classically photo-shopped image at least done tastefully, accentuating the shadows of his cheek and pelvic bones. He looked smoking hot.

Sitting up straight, I managed to catch Charlie before he'd reached the door.

"Charlie," I said. "I'm pretty sure there's going to be a party this afternoon at the office. Want to come?"

"Obviously," he said. "Want me to bring anything?"

"About that," I said. "Is it too late to place a custom cake order?"

I tried calling Eli thrice while perusing the shops, looking for a nice dress to wear. I didn't feel like being surprised, so I straight-out asked Adam if there was going to be a party. Yes, yes there was. Dress code: casual. There was going to be alcohol.

I found a little baby-blue dress that was just slutty enough to illicit a sexy sort-of-confidence when I checked myself out in the mirror, but not so skimpy that it would feel in bad taste at a work event.

I tousled my hair. I put on a bit of lip gloss. I sucked in my stomach, then decided to cut that shit out. I smiled – big, broad, proud. I was proud. I *did it*. I was in print. Who knows who might read the piece? I had no idea where things would go. The sky seemed the limit, truly.

I called Eli again; no answer. I remembered his meeting with the movie suits and then realized I was probably being obnoxious. I'd try again later. I'd invite him to the party. We'd celebrate in the evening, with my new dress and a few drinks.

And a big ol' slice of phallic-shaped confectionary.

It was so strange to finally be in this place. If someone had told teenager-Bailey, with my acne and flaring freckles and unruly hair, sick with self-judgement and poor self-esteem, that I would be working for a notable magazine, with a trendy office – my *own* office – I would dismiss the idea as meant for another Bailey. If someone were to tell me that I'd be in print, able to hand out literal copies of my own work, I would straight-up shoot the notion down. No blank bullets. I'd make sure the gun was loaded.

If someone told me that I'd be living in Los Angeles, driving by the Hollywood sign, wearing a sexy dress and truly feeling myself, I'd think they were insane. Young Bailey believed in her future consisting of a taupe-colored cubicle with a Cutest Puppies calendar tacked-up on the wall, and a cork board covered in motivational quotes and computer print-outs of Orlando Bloom. Maybe a few pictures of the old family dog, Chelsea, a round-but-happy Yellow Lab. I'd wear blouses from Forever21 and straighten my hair and wear heavy jackets during the winter. I'd buy burnt coffee from the corner vendors in their ice-cream-looking trucks, and look straight past every passerby. I'd probably still be living with my mother, and the doily bed-spread, making sure the bed was made every morning and that I kept the curtains dusted. Maybe I'd date – the occasional date with a fellow office co-worker, that never went anywhere, because there wasn't the right chemistry. My job would consist of something administrative, maybe working with numbers and Excel files. I'd go for drinks on the weekends, but end up drinking seltzer and lime. And I'd never leave New Jersey. I'd never even see the West Coast. I'd convince myself it was too easy-breezy, too far-fetched, and I didn't even like the beach that much, anyway. I would try and write on the evenings and weekends, but probably wouldn't end up writing much at all. What would there be in my life worth writing about?

Standing in the elevator, waiting for my floor, poised in my cork wedges and smelling of strawberry body spritzer, I felt a vague pang – a throwback – to my youth. To all the times I told myself that I wasn't an actual writer. It was a pipe-dream. I was just one in a sea of millions that wanted this – the chance to be seen, for my work to be seen – but what did that mean, anyway? I was just one person, and the universe does not care about the individual's hopes and dreams. We're all just scrambling up that wobbly, unstable ladder, hoping for something. Someone.

And I had both: something. Someone.

Elijah Mattox.

The elevator dinged, and the doors opened. I scurried down the hall, spotting Charlie by the entrance. He was still wearing his work clothes. Somehow, this felt appropriate.

"There's booze in there," Charlie noted. "I'll bet five bucks at least a handful of your colleagues are completely loaded right now."

"Make it ten bucks," I told him. "I bet there's at least

twenty folks in there with a hard buzz."

I opened the door, welcomed with a loud, roaring applause. Charlie, who was holding the cake, set it down on a nearby table and immediately dove towards the cocktail bar.

Deborah hugged me, smelling of that same lovely powdered rose and peony. Her smile was bright and her sleek, red Louboutin pumps fabulous.

"Is Eli joining us?" Deb asked. "Or is your man preoccupied?"

I shrugged lightly.

"I haven't been able to reach him, but I think he's held up with movie business. I sent him a text about the party. In the meantime, who's making the cocktails?"

I had no reason to think that anything was amiss. I had no reason to second-guess the few sideways glances, the subtle murmurs, or the sudden lift of his eyebrows – Charlie's eyebrows – which was a thing he always did when he was concerned. Like one of those flash-expressions. He was talking to Adam, and I saw it, quick as lightening. When he caught me looking, he turned away.

I kept drinking my pineapple and Malibu. There were finger-foods – sandwiches, cookies, cheese and fruit trays. I kept myself preoccupied by plating up grapes and melon and thick slices of Gruyère. I had another drink. I chatted with my colleagues about how I felt about the article – finally confessing that I hadn't actually *read* it yet.

"Wait," one said, stunned. "It's almost 5 o'clock, and

you haven't read it? Are you shitting me?"

I shook my head, and I suppose was equally as surprised with myself as the rest were.

I guess the thing of it was – I wrote the article. I knew what was in it. There was something satisfying in that knowledge alone.

There was also an element of anxiety, truth be told. Like an actor that refuses to watch his own films. I was nervous at the thought of actually seeing my words alive on the page.

Besides, what more could holding the actual magazine copy in my hands provide?

But I was so wrong. Perhaps it was still that ghost of my youth telling me that I didn't need to fully indulge in this moment – settling was sufficient. How could I be so conceited as to immediately read my own work? Do I really think that highly of myself?

I tingled holding the glossy, beautiful cover in my hands. There he was – my man, on the cover. My heart pitter-pattered. I could barely breathe. This was it.

This was my work, in the flesh.

And then, I clammed up. I couldn't do it. I was too nervous. What was wrong with me?

"I'll – I'll read it in a minute," I said, holding the magazine to my chest. "Honestly? I'm so tired from the whole process that I kind of just want to enjoy this moment kicking back with you guys and having a few drinks."

So that's what I did: I drank, maybe a little too much. I wasn't hammered, but beyond buzzed. I had a huge slice of cake, sang karaoke with the group, and danced with Deborah to Robyn's *Honey.* We had music. We had alcohol. We had the collective joy of a hundred gleaming faces – some colleagues, but most not. I had the built-up anticipation and thrill of this release that was finally just that – released. It was a straight dose of good, good vibes, and I was feeling it.

Until suddenly, I wasn't.

I was outside, on Deb's office deck, enjoying the warm breeze, my fourth pineapple Malibu in-hand, when I finally heard him speak:

"Bailey," Eli said. "I'm sorry if I'm late."

I spun around, and there he was. My Eli. He smelled of oak and sage. He wore his usual jeans and a T-shirt, his hair a purposeful mess, his eyes slightly shadowed – he seemed tired. And there was no smile on his face, to the point where I stopped mid-step, pausing before hugging him.

"Are you okay?" I asked. "I'm so happy you're here. I've been trying to reach you, but was afraid I was being obnoxious. I know you've got movie stuff. I don't want to be a nudge."

Eli was quiet for a minute – a solid, agonizing minute. He glanced behind him, at the spinning, swirling party. When he turned to me, he looked pained. Hurt.

"How could you write what you did about us?" he asked quietly. "About me? If I'd known, I would have never consented. Maybe this is my fault. I should have read the copy beforehand. I should have taken you up on your offer. I just..."

"Wait, excuse me?" I stammered. I could feel my drink slipping – I set it quickly aside. "I'm confused."

"Confused?" he snapped. "I'm asking how you could write about me like I'm just some – some fucking *playboy*. Some typical, broody, smutty playboy. And our relationship? Was this just a gimmick to you? Was this just for views, or to impress your publisher?"

I was spinning. I felt myself sitting down on the seat behind me. Suddenly, the warm air felt hot – too hot. I wanted to go inside. I had drank too fucking much. I had bought a new dress and a dick cake and even had my hair done-up – but in less than sixty seconds, I felt so stupid. So at-sea.

"I didn't write anything that I wouldn't be okay with you reading," I finally choked out. I insisted. "I swear. I meant what I said."

"So you thought I would – what – appreciate that bullshit?" he asked. "This fucking hurts, Bailey."

"How could you think I'd ever want to hurt you?"

My throat was closing. I was nearly crying. I was dizzy, and out of my head. I was out of my goddamn *realm*.

Eli softened. He blinked, standing quietly, seeming as if attempting to put the broken fragments together. I thought about the piece of artwork, made from broken glass, hanging in Fleur's pantry.

"Did you read the piece?" he asked. "Have you read it yet?"

"No," I confessed. "I haven't read it yet. I was – I don't know. I was waiting for you. I wanted to celebrate tonight with you. I thought this was going to be a happy day. I even – I bought this dress..."

I could feel the tears running, and I wanted nothing but Eli to come and hold me, brush the hair from my face, wipe away the tears, kiss my forehead. I wanted his warmth. I needed it.

Instead, he seemed uncomfortable. When I looked up at him, he looked away.

"Maybe you should talk to your boss," he finally said. "I'm sorry, Bailey. I need to go and clear my head. I'll call you later. We can get a late dinner, if you want."

I could feel the hairline-fracture in my heart; I couldn't take much more of this. I wanted to be bold, of course. I wanted to stand up to him – to stand my ground, to insist that there *must* have been a mistake, and that I'd talk to Deb, and that things would be sorted out – but I had no idea what I was doing. I had no idea what had transpired between this morning – hell, from when I sent the final draft to Deb – and now. Had I been deceived somehow?

I watched, helpless, as Eli left. Countless sets of eyes fell on him, then fell away. Whispers. Gossip. Glances to me, standing outside, disheveled, tear-stained.

Eventually Charlie found me. He handed me a bottle of water and hugged me, as if he knew something I didn't.

"You should read the article," he said, his tone soft but serious. "Sit down."

I still had a copy of the magazine next to me, being used thoughtlessly as a coaster for my now watered-down drink. I picked it up, sat down, and flipped to the story piece.

Charlie crouched down next to me, waiting while I read.

First glance: it was much shorter than what I'd written.

Second read-through: it was not only revised, but completely butchered. No mention of Eli's past, or my past, or the nuance of our many, many feelings. The sweet nothings shared and the stunning intimacy, was laying somewhere on the cold cutting floor.

In it's place was, frankly, trash. A virgin. A porn star. A fucking joke. I was painted as the ditsy, curious, pining virgin. Eli was nothing but a fuck-toy that got a lucky break.

But hey, the ending? We were in item. We were a thing. Oh, how *adorable*.

It was cheap. The entire piece was disgustingly cheap. It wasn't even recognizable as something I had written. A stranger had written this. Tampered – all of my work had been tampered with, bleached-stained. I might as well have written nothing.

I dropped the magazine, stood, and stormed into the office. I found Deb standing by the bar, tilting back a martini, her smile glimmering. When she saw me, she set her drink aside.

"Bailey?" she asked. "What's wrong, love?"

"What...what did you do?" I asked. I implored. I begged. "What happened to the final draft I submitted? I don't even recognize what's in that fucking magazine.

That isn't mine."

"Adam took an editorial pass at it, and made some necessary revisions," she stated plainly. "It's nothing personal, Bailey. Just about everything that we publish goes through a heavy-handed editing. Surely you understood that."

"You didn't even give me the chance to read the final draft before you set it out into the wild!" I exclaimed. "Who does that?"

Her smile dropped.

"Do you need a water?" she asked, as if *I* was the one who didn't get it. As if this was just some grand overreaction, and as if I should have anticipated this. I should have expected it. How could I not have expected it? Bailey Finch: forever naive. "Do you want to go somewhere a little more quiet and talk?"

"No," I said. "But I'd like to know – who else has had their work completely fucking butchered for the sake of a smutty magazine?"

My voice was louder than I intended it to be. I could feel Deb's hand on my shoulder, firm. A veiled threat.

A few hands raised, sheepish. A few more hands slid up, questioning. There was a tight, quiet air.

I sucked in a slow breath. How could I not have anticipated this? This was the kind of place I was writing for. *Come Magazine*. Of course they were going to make whatever revisions they wanted to craft the kind of story they wanted to tell – which was never of substance. We didn't sell substance – we sold sex.

I was so green. I was green here, at the office, despite

my office upgrade and all of this praise. I should have known, because I had some idea, some understanding. But it was never me – it was never *my* work that was sliced and diced for the sake of catering to our viewer base or publisher's whims.

"I need to leave," I said quietly. "I'm sorry, Deb. I need to leave. I need to get out of here."

Charlie was nearby, his expression unreadable. When we left, he tossed his copy of the magazine in the trash. He told me to do the same, but I couldn't. I clung onto it like a bad breakup letter.

I wept the entire way home. I tried calling Eli. I waited for his call. Nothing.

It felt as if he were already gone, and maybe he was.

Maybe this entire thing was just a big mistake.

Maybe I truly was naive, and didn't know how the world worked, and didn't really understand what it meant to be a writer. Maybe I was just heartbroken, and still a little bit buzzed, and not thinking straight.

Maybe it was all over, and it just hadn't hit me yet. Maybe this was a dream, and I would soon wake up, and none of this had ever actually happened at all.

CHAPTER 14
Goodbye, Stars

Eli didn't call the next day, either. He didn't call me on Saturday, or Sunday. On Monday, I didn't go into work. I hadn't even showered – I couldn't get out of bed. When Deb called, I ignored her. When Charlie knocked on my door, bringing offerings of condolence Chinese, I sent him away, too.

The magazine was covered with water-marks from accidentally spilling a cup of Diet Coke on it. It was sticky, and the pages clung together, but I still managed to ease them apart and let them dry – crinkly to the touch – and spent the better part of the morning and afternoon reading and re-reading the abomination that was my *big break*.

"I quit," I said aloud, to no one. *I quit.*

When Charlie knocked again, I let him in. He brought a plate of fried rice and a can of ginger ale, setting it down on my dresser.

"I'm not hungry," I told him. "I'm stupid."

"You're not stupid," he insisted. "Far from it. What they did to you was shitty. Really shitty. I mean, that isn't even your work at this point. It's not you."

"But am I an idiot?" I asked him, dead serious. "Revisions happen. We don't always have a say in the final result. Did you see how many hands went up when I asked if this had happened to anyone else? How could

I not have known? I was idealistic. It's just...she loved my idea. Deb loved everything I was sending to her. I guess I just assumed she'd be keeping all of it."

"That's enough for the better part of a novel," Charlie chuckled. "I'm not defending them. But it makes sense that some of it would inevitably get cut."

"You know," I said. "Deb had mentioned that. There was enough there for a book. She'd mentioned a publishing company. Higher-powers, she called them. But at this point, I wouldn't want to give her a referral fee. "

"Like, a company that would offer you a legit book deal?"

"I have no idea," I told him. "I actually think she was joking about the referral fee. I don't know. It doesn't matter. I don't want to talk to her."

"You *should*," he said. "Talk to her, I mean. I know Eli is pissed, but you don't want to burn bridges. This is still a huge opportunity, Bail. You don't want to blow it. You know you don't want to blow it."

"Yeah," I sighed.

Charlie stood, grabbed the plate of rice and the ginger ale, and handed them to me.

"You need to *eat*," he insisted. "And then you need to call your boss."

"I will."

"Promise me," his voice was stern, fatherly. It made me smile.

"I promise," I swore.

When he left, I swallowed down the rice and drank

some of the fizzy generic-brand tonic, then slowly got out of bed. I took a shower, dried my hair, dressed. It was slow-moving, sluggish. I felt as if I'd just come out of a coma; as if my blood were moving slowly. I still felt a little dizzy, uncertain, queasy.

Setting everything aside, I called Deb.

We met at a cafe nearby the office. I ordered an iced latte, whole milk. Deb ordered green tea with a spoonful of honey.

She looked tired. I tried to scrutinize her expression – I wanted to feel the same rage, the same fuck-it-all feelings I had felt just a couple days ago. But looking at her, with her makeup-less face, her dark under-eyes, her pursed lips...I couldn't hate her. She looked genuinely beyond herself. She was even wearing flats, and Deb was never seen without a heel.

We didn't speak for a good minute or two. We sat there, awkwardly, sipping at our beverages. It was a warm day, and the caramel-colored sun seeped through the leaves of the trees that lined the sidewalk. The air smelled of roasting coffee and something herbal – eucalyptus. The streets were quiet, save for the bubble-gum teenagers skipping school, skating by in their bubble-gum colored roller skates. They whizzed past, laughing, like simple youth. Like a mist that fell and then evaporated so quickly. I never learned how to skate.

I turned, looked at Deb, stirred around the ice in my

latte.

"I'm not sure how to feel," I said quietly. "Eli is mad. He's really mad. He's hurt, actually, more than anything, but he still hasn't spoken to me. That's what this is really about, I guess, Deb. Your revisions have royally fucked-up my relationship."

Deb nodded, listening. She sighed lightly, looked out past me, towards the trees or maybe the roller skaters, as if she were searching for something. Maybe she was. Maybe she was searching for the words.

"I got Lasik surgery about seven years ago," she eventually said. "Before that, I wore contacts. Before that, I wore glasses. And before that, I went years – well into my teens, actually, not wearing anything at all."

How was this relevant? I said nothing, waiting.

She cleared her throat lightly.

"Anyway, I was a very vain teenager. Shocking, I know. For the longest time, I would get these debilitating migraines – I chalked them up to menstrual migraines for the longest time – until my mother finally brought me in to get my eyes checked, and they told me that I needed glasses. For me, it was terrible news. It was the nineties, and contact lenses weren't an option for me. For starters, I couldn't stick my fingers near my eye, even if my life *depended* on it. Secondly, insurance. It would only cover glasses. So I was stuck."

"What does this have to do with anything?" I felt myself growing irate. I sucked in a sharp breath, forcing patience. "Adam butchered my work, and nobody warned me."

She nodded meekly.

"Bear with me, here," Deb requested. "You know, I fought that doctor for a long time, telling them that I could see just fine, because technically I could – I didn't need glasses for driving, or school-work. Eventually, I caved and got the prescription filled. I picked out a pair of frames. But instead of wearing them, I tucked them away in my purse or hid them in my locker. I thought they made me look horrendous. But the point that I'm getting at is – I finally put them on. I was sitting outside, in the quad, reading a book. It was a beautiful day, a lot like this one, and I was watching the sunlight through the trees, and I just decided, since no one else was around, to put the glasses on. And Bailey, I realized I could see. Really see."

She actually choked up. She took a napkin, blotting her eyes. I couldn't find it in me to say anything.

"I thought things were fine as they were," she continued. "Until I realized what was missing. What I'm trying to say, Bailey, is that I don't want us to be at war, here. You are a fine, talented writer. One of the finest I've met. What's happened with your work was never intended to be a slight, or an offense. I guess we should have spoken more about expectations with a piece of that...well, size. But I don't want you to quit. We don't want to lose you around the office. If I lost you, Bailey, it would be like it was before I decided to start wearing those glasses. Your office would be a blur. Some people are irreplaceable."

I felt stubborn, but my heart still ached.

"That doesn't fix my relationship," I informed her. "I'm sorry, Deb. That was a beautiful monologue. But I don't know if I can come back to work if it means that whatever future writing I submit will need to be rinsed and trimmed to meet the so-called standards of *Come Magazine*. I'm not saying that I don't understand or respect the revision process, but I guess what I'm saying, Deb..." I paused again, taking deep breath. "I don't want to write for your magazine anymore. I can't. I don't want to write about sex, or how to turn someone on while wearing a potato sack, or how to reach climax hanging upside-down like a bat. I want to tell stories."

Deb nodded again, understanding.

"I'm sad," she confessed. "I hope we can still be friendly. I hope you still come and visit us. I hope you can at least forgive Adam for his heavy editorial hand."

"Yeah," I murmured. "Maybe eventually."

She was smiling when I met her gaze again. For a moment, she appeared hesitant, as if holding onto a secret she didn't yet want to give up.

Then, opening her purse, she withdrew from her wallet what appeared to be a business card. There was a name and number scratched on it: Isla Walker, *Silver Crane Publishing*.

"I didn't want to make any assumptions," she told me. "I didn't want to tell them you'd be interested, or take any ownership of your work, in the event you just wanted to move on. But if you're interested, she would love to speak with you."

I took the business card, holding it in my hands

delicately. The text was glossy, the card bone-white, pleasantly-textured to the touch.

"Are you saying they'd want to publish my piece?" I asked. "Like, in a book?"

Deb stood, tousling my hair as if I were her sister, her daughter. There was something familial about it.

"Call them," she told me. "If you want. I need to get back to the office. But Bailey, thank you for meeting with me."

I hugged her, and any begrudging feelings I'd possessed seemed to slowly fall away, like crumbling cement. I became softened, not rigid. I was easing back into myself. Slowly, but surely.

When she walked away, after a few steps, she turned to me again.

"And Bailey?" she said. "I was joking about the referral. You're free."

I'm free. I'm free. What did that mean? I still felt the weight of loss, heavy, like lead. My softness gave way to a sudden wave of grief, but I didn't want to cry right there, in the middle of a quiet cafe, in public.

Instead, I watched Deb walk away, and kept stirring the ice in my drink, and occasionally sipped it. I tried to enjoy the temperate weather in my short-sleeved blouse, the light breeze, the lazy warmth of the sun. Eventually I finished my latte and ordered another, opting to go inside and hopeful that my blues might be eased by a little coffee shop music. There was a table open, next to the window, so I could still see the trees.

I pictured Eli, standing there, outside the window, his

sarcastic smile crookedly charming. I closed my eyes and tried to remember all of the good moments – the good feelings. The thrill of the sex club, sitting with our feet in the sand on the beach, being hand-fed spicy scallops at hole-in-the-wall restaurants with names I couldn't pronounce, with tea lights dangling from the roof like little stars.

I tried to remember stars. I tried to remember the feeling of his lips against mine, soft and rough and tender all at once, and how Eli would look at me as if I were the only woman on the planet that ever had and ever would exist. I was the only thing that mattered.

I rested my head against the table-top, my temples throbbing. My brain was so murky that all of the memories came back in bits and pieces, like static television. I tried to shake my head, change the channel, beg the wiring in my brain to straighten out. But nothing. Everything was a jumbled mess.

And then, I felt a tap on my shoulder. Head heavy, I lifted my chin to look at who was standing next to me, suddenly brimming with hope. Eli. *Eli, Eli. Eli.*

It wasn't Eli. In fact, I didn't immediately recognize who was standing in front of me. Light red-blond hair, a dewy complexion, a few dainty freckles on the tip of her nose. Her doe-like eyes were wide, her lashes even longer with mascara. She wore a white tank top and acid-washed hip-hugger jeans, accentuating her slim curves. Her pony tail bounced as she jostled, appearing nervous, her arms crossed, which only succeeded in suggestively pressing her breasts together.

Then, it clicked. This was Cora. Cora from the party. Cora from the bathtub. Eli's ex-girlfriend.

"Cora," I said, softer than intended. "What can I do for you?"

"Can I buy you a coffee?" she asked, then noted the coffee already sitting in front of me. "Or another one? Something else?"

"I'm fine," I said. My voice felt raspy, tired. "Did you need something?"

She teetered back and forth on her feet, swaying lightly. She looked uncertain, disquieted, restless. This was uncomfortable for the both of us.

"I guess I just saw you, and was surprised," she finally said. She was quiet for a moment longer before finally adding: "How is Eli?"

Gone. Gone, like dust in the wind. Instead, not wanting to give the idea that there was any availability, because I was a petty bitch, I said:

"He's doing okay," I said. "We're doing okay. Long week."

"Looks that way," she said. "Could I sit down?"

"If you want."

She seated herself across from me, brushing the hair from her eyes and taking a few moments to just look at me. It was an unreadable expression – confusion, sadness, envy. A mix of things, really.

It didn't seem as if she didn't like me. But Cora regarded me, seemingly, as if I were a mistake. As if Eli didn't actually see the same Bailey that everyone else did. Heavy-set and undefined, with flat hair and mismatching eyeliner.

"I'm sorry about the party," she finally said. "I made a real fool of myself."

"It's nothing. I'm glad you're alright," I said, which was true. I didn't wish her any harm. "I'm sorry if I upset you, being there with Eli. I'm sorry I lied about who I was to him."

She was quiet again. I'd unintentionally struck a weak cord.

"It's been hard," she confessed. With just three words, I could feel myself instantly leaning into the conversation. A conversation I didn't really want to have, with a person I didn't want to be sitting in front of, but haven't you been there before, too? You don't want it, and yet you do. You want whatever is about to transpire to blow up so, *so* badly. Like the temptation to jump off a bridge, into open water. I needed to crash. "I miss him."

"Yeah," I blinked. "Break-ups can be hard. They're never easy."

Cora tapped a lacquered finger against the table. She was so ridiculously pretty, like a water sprite. I tried to fight the desire to stare when I realized she wasn't wearing a bra – her breasts, large and round, were just that weightless. I guessed they weren't real.

"Did he ever mention me?" she finally asked. This is what she'd wanted to ask, I realized. This is what Cora wanted to know – what every ex probably wants to know, deep down. Have they been mentioned? What was said? Does he still think about me? The human ego knows no bounds. "I mean, did he ever talk about us?"

"Not really," I told her. I refrained from adding that it was only because he'd told me there was not much to talk about. They weren't that serious. She was just jilted – a typical jilted ex. Not that this settled comfortably with me. I hated the label of *jilted ex.* It felt gross. "Not really at all, actually. I'm sorry. I know that's kind of blunt."

She pressed her lips together. I watched her throat move as if in pain.

"He might still be grieving," she said. "It was a lot to get over."

And there I was, further leaning in. Did I really want to know what she was talking about?

"Breakups can take awhile," I found myself repeating. I decided to indulge her. "Maybe he is still getting over it. I don't know all of Eli's past."

"We were going to have a baby," she said, out of the blue, as if mentioning that it were a nice day outside, or that the coffee here was unconscionably expensive. As if it were a passive fact. She wasn't even looking at me, but rather out the window. Far, far away. "I mean, we lost the baby. But we were together for a couple years when it happened. We're both in the industry – well, I guess Eli is past-tense, now. But when I got pregnant, he was going to marry me. When I miscarried..."

She paused, took another breath. My skin had gone cold. I struggled to process exactly what she was saying:

They were together for years. More than a single year. Years.

She was pregnant with his baby.

He was going to marry her.

He was going to marry Cora.

"When I miscarried," she continued. "I broke it off with him. I couldn't look at him. We still had to work together, which was hard, but eventually it became easier. I took a break for awhile, got myself together. I really thought I was over him, but I guess...I guess it does take awhile. I'm sorry if this is all coming off as just a random, crazy outburst. I'm not insane, I swear."

"I believe you," I said, arguably emotionless. "I'm so sorry that happened."

"Yeah," she said quietly. "Me too. But I'm glad to know he's doing well. I'm glad to know he seems to have moved on. You seem like a nice girl."

"Thank you," I said. "That's kind of you to say."

The words felt sterile and lifeless. I wanted her to go away. I had nothing else to say – nothing else I could say. I had no energy for words. I just wanted to sink down into my chair and enter into a comatose state until I could wake up a fully-functioning human woman. I wished my heart were made of iron. I wished it wasn't beating at all.

"It was nice to see you, Cora," I eventually said. "But if you don't mind, I'm in the middle of some work. I really need to get back to it."

I had no paper, pen, or laptop in front of me. I'm not sure if she could tell that this was a blatant lie. She didn't fight it, however. Cora instead stood, and smiled weakly, and thanked me again. For a second, it looked as if she were going to offer a hug, but then she slowly withdrew, turned, and hustled out the door.

I could still smell her perfume after she'd gone – something woodsy, earthy, purchased from some New Age kiosk downtown where they sold incense and prayer candles.

I sat in my chair, still as a statue. I wanted to cry, but the tears weren't there. My insides felt heavy, chalky, dry. I could barely breathe.

Eli had lied to me, so it seemed. I was not the first serious woman he had dated. I wasn't the first serious romance. He had loved and lost before – more than just a woman. A baby. Eli would have been a father. Maybe he still considered himself to be; the father of a ghost-child he would never meet. God, how bleak was that?

I felt so cold. I felt defeated. I didn't even care about the magazine anymore, or about my writing, or about being a writer. I felt as if I'd lost a piece of myself. Before meeting Eli, I would have scolded this scene as pathetic – how could you lose yourself over a guy, or any relationship? Not worth it. Stand up, chin up. The whole *girl, wash your face* bullshit.

It didn't matter then, though. When you fall in love, all logic goes straight out the window. I couldn't control it. All I could do was watch it slip from my hands, like those grains of sand on the beach.

Goodbye, stars.

I didn't bother calling him again, or sending another text. Like a mad-woman, I drove to his house, where the gate was open, and went straight to his door. I knocked, loudly, my throat growing tighter with every slam of my fist.

Eventually, Eli opened the door. He looked as if he'd just woken up – sleepy, groggy, heavy-lidded. He didn't seem surprised to see me, but rather inconvenienced. As if I were the mailman. As if I were a UPS driver that delivered a package to the wrong address. As if I were a stranger, and had the wrong house.

"Can I come in?" I asked, feeling the words begin to spill. "Please?"

He stood aside, to my surprise, letting me in. But he said nothing.

In the foyer, standing with my arms crossed, I felt my heart pound. I was angry. My heart was broken. But standing there, in front of him, I still felt so weak.

"I saw Cora," I said shakily. "At a coffee shop. She came up to me, and started talking to me. And before you say anything, I didn't instigate this. I had gone to the shop to meet up with my boss, to demand an explanation for the magazine piece that was so heavily edited, Eli, it wasn't what I actually *wrote*. That wasn't *me.*"

I was winded, rambling, my breathing heavy. From my bag, I withdrew a manilla envelope, heavy with paper. I tossed it on the floor, in front of his feet.

"*That*," I said. "Is what I wrote. That's all of it. You can take it or leave it, but that's my piece. Not what's in the magazine, although I can't apologize enough for how much they gutted my writing. You need to know that my heart is broken too, Eli.”

And there they were – the tears. The tears started flowing.

“My heart is broken, too,” I repeated. “And Cora. She came up to me, and started asking about you, and then before I could even get a word out she started talking about how *serious* you two were, and how you got her pregnant, and how she broke it off with you after she had a miscarria-”

“Bailey,” Eli was suddenly alert. His eyes were two live wires. “Cora spoke with you?”

“Are you listening to me?” I snapped. “Yes. Yes. And apparently, you're a fucking liar. Apparently you've been lying to me this entire time. Telling me that I'm the first serious woman you've been with, as if I need to hear that, because I'm a virgin, right? I'm too sensitive, too fragile, to be able to comprehend you having loved another woman, apparently. Well, Eli, I might be a virgin, but I'm not a china doll. And I might have low self-esteem – I might have terrible self-esteem, actually – but for fuck's sake, I can handle the thought of you having dated another woman. I can handle Eli with a past. I mean, look at your past! I've been handling your past since we first met, and I still – I still love you, Eli.”

I was weeping. I swept past him, feeling him follow me into the living room, where I sank down into the sofa like a dead weight. He sat down next to me, carefully. He didn't touch me. He said nothing.

“How could you dare lie to me, and then ignore me

because you're pissed off about a piece of writing? You didn't even bother to talk to me about it, Eli. You just...you shut me out. You sent me away."

"Bailey," he said. I brushed him off.

"How could you lie, and then dare say that you love me?" I demanded. "You don't love me. You don't know what loving someone even is. I'm not sure I do, either. This was just a bad story. This was never meant to have a happy ending. We both just got swept up in the idea of us."

"Is that what you really think?" he asked. "Could I tell you something?"

"I don't care what you have to say," I said, stubborn. Hard-headed. "Fine. Fine, say whatever you want."

I was hiccuping. I was a mess. A total mess. Eyeliner streaming down my cheeks, lips bitten, all of it.

"Cora was never pregnant," he said carefully. "She told me she was. But did you know that when I took her to the doctor, trying to be supportive – because I won't pretend that I wasn't trying to be supportive – the doctor told her that she wasn't pregnant. He ran the blood work. He did an ultrasound. There was no baby, Bailey. The positive pregnancy test was from a chemical pregnancy – but nothing was ever actually lost."

"Then explain what Cora was telling me," I said, hardened. I didn't believe him.

"I can't say for sure," he said. "Maybe she left a test sitting for too long, and thought she saw a false positive. Maybe the doctor's explanation of a chemical pregnancy was the right one. Maybe I'm just fucking man-splaining this whole thing, and shouldn't be saying anything at all. All I know is that she wasn't pregnant."

"She said you were going to marry her."

"Yes," he confessed. "For a moment, when I believed she was pregnant, I told her we could get married. But it wasn't a proposal, Bailey. She was all over the place. She was devastated. I was...trying to do what I thought was right. Upstanding. I was an unplanned pregnancy. I didn't want her to be alone like my mother was."

He shook his head, turning away.

"I never really loved her," he swore, as if that's what I needed to hear. The most pathetic part was that I did, in all truth. I needed to hear that he never loved her. I was insecure and all bare wires, sparking wildly, unhinged. "But I loved you, Bailey."

I sat quietly, pulling at the threads of my shirt, still processing.

"You said it wasn't serious," I said. "But she said you guys were together for a couple years. That's not nothing, Eli. Even just imagining a pregnancy, or promising marriage, isn't casual."

"It can be," he said, and there was truth in the weight of his words. "It can be casual. Anything can be casual, and anything can have meaning. We assign to relationships – to people, to anything – whatever we want to. As for Cora, I didn't love her. I could tell you this in a million different ways, but I didn't, and we weren't together for a couple years. We were fucking, on and off again, for a couple years. There was never hearts, or flowers, or dates. She wasn't you, Bailey."

"You think that's what I want to hear?" I said, but it was. It so was. "I'm a stronger woman than that."

But I wasn't. Maybe that was okay.

I looked at Eli again, who nodded, his eyes soft, heart-broken as I was.

"I was going to call you when I woke up," he insisted. "I just needed to rest. I've been really on-edge. With this movie, with us...sometimes, I guess I doubt myself, too. These big directors, they see something in me. Something worth starring in this film with a horrendously massive budget. I'm going to be on the big-screen. I stand a chance at people knowing me as someone other than Elijah Mattox – part-time human, as you once said. I won't just be a porn star, anymore. I've tried to pretend like the fact that people see me as an object doesn't bother me, but it does. You though, Bailey, you've always seen me. And I love you."

He started crying. Soft, gentle heaves. He covered his face with his hands, his chest lightly heaving, his breathing jagged.

"I wish I could just run away with you," he said. "I wish we could just run away and get married and pretend like none of the pain ever happened. I'm so sorry I've hurt you. I don't want you to hurt, Bailey."

Eli hugged me, like a desperate child, his arms tight around me, my face against his chest. I could feel his heart pounding, the thrum like a thick guitar string snapping. Like something ending.

We pulled away, kissed each other gently, softly, our lips barely brushing.

"Marry me," he said, wiping a stray tear from my cheek.

I wiped a tear away from his cheek, kissing him again. I kissed him again, and again, feeling the anger begin to slowly melt, and feeling myself slowly begin to melt into him, until we were both desperately holding each other. We were soft, and gentle, and my hands were on his face, and I couldn't stop looking at him – at this stunning man, with the sad eyes and sunken cheekbones, his hair a mess, looking like a lost puppy who was trying to find home. I've heard it said that sometimes home is a place – other times, it's a person.

"I love you," he said. I tried not to hear the pain in his voice. "Marry me."

"You don't know what you're asking," I said softly. "You don't want to marry me."

What I couldn't tell him: I had called Isla, in New York. She was interested in my story, except she indeed had the idea for a novel. This was to be something bigger, in print, on bookshelves. This time next year, if all went seamlessly, I would see my book in the windows of book shops. I would be an author.

I was leaving tomorrow. I couldn't tell him that, either. All I could do was let him look at me, so mournfully, and weep against his chest, trying to pretend that I wasn't breaking, and that I wasn't the type of girl to feel this much pain over a man, and that I didn't need him.

I tried to believe the lies.

CHAPTER 15
Home Is Where You Are

I took Charlie along with me to New York. Until my invitation, he had never left the West Coast. On the plane ride, he talked about all the things he'd never seen – snow, for starters. He'd never seen an actual New England autumn. He'd never traveled to watch the leaves turn, or went sledding as a child, or built a snowman.

"I hate the cold," he confessed, shrugging. "I don't know how much I'd actually enjoy living on the East Coast versus the idea I have of what it would be like to build a snowman."

"There's always a vacation," I suggested. "You don't have to live on the East Coast to build a snowman. Just visit for a few days. You could go outside, look at the snow, and then return to your AirBnb cabin and relax in temperature-controlled bliss."

Our flight landed late at night. Still, the city was bustling. Charlie had his camera out, snapping photos of the neon-colored lights and the skyscrapers, tall enough to graze the skyline. The air was dirty, thick, filled with billowing smoke from the underground. But this was nothing we weren't used to – LA air isn't exactly clean. We were used to the burning in our lungs. I guess we were even fine with it.

"I want to see everything," he gushed. "I want to see those giant statues of M&Ms and eat a real New York slice. I want to go to Central Park. I want to see a Broadway show."

"A Broadway show might be a stretch this last-minute," I told him. "But let's check into our hotel, and I can do something about getting you a real New York slice."

So we checked into our hotel, The Knickerbocker, tossed our luggage on the floor, and then decided to head straight out in search for pizza. There was a Joe's nearby, and we shared two pies – one with fresh-sliced mozzarella, thick and melty – and Pepperoni, Charlie's favorite. We ate until we were so full that we could barely move around in our seats. We drank Coke from the can, carbonated and overly sweet. I felt a warm buzz, from the city and the lights and the one-too-many slices of pizza, even though I hadn't had a sip of alcohol.

I loved the city. I loved the way it was always breathing, no matter the hour, kept alive by the thousands and thousands of inhabitants, both local and from countries or states I'd never see for myself.

I took a drink of Coke, sighing heavily. My chest still ached. I still missed Eli, and was trying like hell to shove him far, far away from my thoughts. I needed this trip to fit into a specific box – this was about the book. This was about me, and my writing, and certainly something I should be damned excited about.

But Eli was a part of this story – I couldn't shake him.

I missed him so much.

"Do you think you'll move here?" Charlie asked, cutting through my stream of a million different thoughts. "To New York, I mean. You'd be closer to your Mom. You'd be in a city where you didn't need to drive everywhere. You'd have seasons back."

"I don't know," I confessed. "Maybe? I'm not sure. I love LA. LA has become my home. I'd miss the warmth, and the cypress trees, and your coffee shop. I'd miss seeing you all the time, in any case."

"I'm not going to be working at that coffee shop forever," Charlie reminded me. "But I know. I'd miss seeing you every day, too. I'd need to find a new roommate. It's hard, starting over."

I took a sharp breath. I felt a pang in my heart.

"Yeah," I agreed. "Yeah. Yeah, it is."

"Are you going to tell Eli that you're in New York?" he asked. "Are you obligated to tell him about the book? Does he need to sign a release or anything for you to publish it?"

"Not if I change his name, tweak some things. You know, create a fiction piece out of non-fiction. People do it all the time. I don't need his permission to tell a story, even if it's heavily influenced by him."

"Do you want to tell the truth, though?" he asked. "I'd rather tell the actual story. I'd rather go in knowing things are pure."

"Things were never *pure*," I reminded him. "Our relationship was completely nonsensical from the beginning. Did you know he asked me to marry him yesterday?"

"You're kidding me," Charlie sat back in his seat, eyes wide. "Elijah Mattox asked you to marry him – and he was serious?”

"Dead serious," I told Charlie. "Tears and all. He was practically begging me to marry him."

"And do...did you want to say yes?"

Yes. No. Yes. I swallowed.

"A part of me wanted to say yes. Is that *insane*?" I asked him. "But I said no, of course, because it would have been insane. I don't even know why I'm asking if it would have been insane. We both have too much baggage. We barely know each other, anyway."

"My grandparents knew each other for a month before they got married," Charlie offered. "I'm not sure if there's a right way to go about these things. You know, in your gut, and you just go for it. Setting aside, you know, obvious dysfunction. Obvious red-flags. But I don't think that's what you and Eli were dealing with, Bails. You've both just been in pain. A lot of pain. Everyone has a past, but you know, everyone is entitled to a future. A future where they're happy."

"What are you saying, exactly?"

"I'm saying that you deserve to be happy," he was serious, pointed. "You're not nuts for having a flash-thought of marrying Eli. People could date for a decade, get married, and call it quits a month later. People can get married, like my grandparents, after a month and spend sixty-years, happily, together. There's no use trying to do the right thing, or else you'll spend your whole life over-thinking and wasting precious time."

"You're quite the philosopher these days," I smiled.

"I have way too much time on my hands, is all,"

Charlie chuckled. "I read a lot of books for a guy with Justin Bieber posters on my bedroom walls, believe it or not. Also, my therapist told me most of this. This is free therapy, bitch."

"Free therapy, eh?"

We both laughed, lightly, the noise quickly evaporating amidst the sound of the crowded shop – the many folks, families, homeless, even, coming in for a simple slice of pizza. We were all just looking for that feeling of fullness – a hunger, satiated.

And I was still hungry, despite my stomach being full. Eli wasn't here. I'd left him, to get on a plane, to find myself in New York, to sign a book deal that I'd never even told him about. I was keeping secrets, too.

The biggest: I loved him. I loved him, and his broken past, and his million mistakes, and his flaws. I loved the way he looked at me, and the way he grinned, and the way he was just like me, in so many ways. He was just a guy, like I was just a girl, and we were fighting against this raging riptide, together.

"I'm just afraid of making a big mistake, and getting hurt, or hurting him," I told Charlie. "I don't want to hurt anyone else. I don't want to hurt, either."

"You're going to, at some point or another, over something," Charlie said. "It might as well be risked over something – someone – that matters to you. Yeah, I know that's cheesy as all hell. But it's true, and you know it."

He was right. He usually was.

I reached out for a final slice of pizza, biting into it,

chewing thoughtfully.

"You're smarter than people give you credit for," I told him. "I guess by people, I mean myself. I'm sorry I never came to you more often."

"Here's to starting over," Charlie raised his can, and I raised mine, and we toasted to something new, and unknown. We toasted to whatever was to come.

The publishing house was small, with potted plants and floor-to-ceiling windows overlooking the black and white and gold of the surrounding buildings that almost seemed to blur with one another. It seemed a watercolor, almost, all the moving people below. From up high in the skyline, they looked like a blend of paint droplets, and not much else.

It was a small office, intimate, and smelled of juniper potpourri. I inked a contract sitting in a small room, with a shaky hand, and an even shakier handshake. I tried to muster the same confidence I had when I was working with Deb – I wore a suit, I styled my hair, I tried to smile the right way – but I was plagued with worry that I still came off as a total hack. Depression had brought my self-esteem issues reeling back, loud as roaring thunder, and it was all I could hear. Not, *you're hilarious, you're charming*, or *you're writing is real.* I heard my own heart-beat, and saw the micro-expressions of disappointment, doubt, distaste in my outfit or my hairstyle or me, in general. I left the office excited, in a sense, but also feeling as uncertain of myself as perhaps

I had ever felt.

Of all things, I called my mother. I wanted to see if she would make the trek into the city to meet me for lunch. I realized, I needed to talk to her. I needed to talk to her a long time ago. But now was better than never.

To my surprise, she agreed. We met at a small Italian restaurant that served a strong Tom Collins, and all the tables had red-and-white checkered tablecloth. A violinist played, table-to-table, and a thick, melted wax candle sat stuck in an old wine bottle, as the table's centerpiece. I ordered chicken piccatta, and she ordered a glass of Chardonnay and a Caprese salad – not that this was what our meeting was about. The food itself was irrelevant, the atmosphere perhaps too intimate. Maybe I should have chosen another location. Was it too late to change my mind?

"Mom," I decided to just dive in. There was no other way to do this. "I'm really glad you made the drive to meet me. That means a lot."

"Of course, honey," my mother's words were candied, sincere, even though all of my million neurosis were screaming at me that her words were anything *but*. She didn't want to be here – this was a politeness, not a gesture of love. "You picked a beautiful spot."

"The violinist is perhaps a bit much," I offered. I took advantage of a moment to smile lightly. "I've got to tell you something, though. I kind of just want to spit it out. It might hurt, but please know, I'm not wanting to hurt you, Mom. I'm sorry if I do."

I shook my head, correcting myself.

"Actually," I continued. "I'm not sorry if I do. But I'm sorry if you don't like what I have to say."

My mother sat up, straightened. I expected a look of disinterest, of inconvenience. How could I have asked her to drive into the city, with the traffic and the dirty air, just to rip her a new one? How selfish of me, how thoughtless. What kind of daughter was I? What kind of daughter would do this to their aging mother? Didn't I understand how bad the roads were? Didn't I understand the severity of my mother's current plumbing situation at home? The plumber was once again there, by himself, alone in the house. Anything could happen. I wasn't even considering the ancient dishware in her china cabinet or her jewelry box, sitting atop her dresser, vulnerable.

Instead, she appeared concerned.

"What is it, honey?" she asked.

"It's a lot of things," I started. "But mainly, I just wanted to let you know, with complete transparency, that growing up with you was really hard. It was hard enough to be in an untraditionally-attractive body, or a generally untraditionally-attractive person. It was hard enough, struggling with my natural weight, without you chastising me, and pushing all those diets, and constantly nit-picking my every move. I grew up feeling inadequate, is the truth. I grew up not feeling good enough. Despite the good grades, and the extra-curriculars, and this book deal – I just signed a book deal, Mom. An excellent one. This time next year, I'll be a published author, with a book on the shelves. I'll have something I could sign an autograph in. And I should be so proud of this, but..."

I could feel a lump form in my throat. I took a moment. I didn't want to cry.

"...I walked out of that office today, and I felt like shit. All I could think about was how weird my body looked in the suit I was wearing, or that my hair looked flat, or that there was no way my ex-boyfriend could have ever really wanted me, because who could really want me, looking like I do, and with my thousands of insecurities? Frankly, Mom, I was borderline suicidal, growing up. I thought about a lot of dark alternatives. I struggled to see myself as anything other than a pudgy fuck-up. You had so many lines in the sand, Mom. Hard lines, and the lines were always changing. I never knew where I could step. I never knew what I could eat, or say, or do. I felt unlovable. And that – that, Mom – was hard. I'm sorry to just spill all of this on you, right here, but I had to finally say something, because it's been suffocating me. And I don't want to die, Mom. I don't want to live feeling like this anymore."

My mother was quiet for a long time. She drank her wine, requested another glass, poked at the grape tomatoes on her dish, but didn't eat. I couldn't tell what she was thinking, or feeling, and a part of that scared me. I wanted to know that I had reached her – not hurt her – just reached her. That she understood. That she saw me.

Finally, she spoke.

"I'm so sorry," she said quietly. "It's hard to find the

right words. But you are right, and I failed you in a lot of ways. I didn't start off with the intention of harming you, or inflicting all of this pain, but I did. I simply did. I couldn't keep myself in-check. I didn't take ownership for the pain I was feeling in my own life, and Bailey, there was a lot of it. I loved your father. I wanted to feel in control of my life – I wanted to feel loved. Instead, I tried to take control in all the wrong ways, believing I was helping, believing I was being a good mother. But I wasn't, Bailey. I know I wasn't. And I'm so sorry that this is where we've ended.”

“It doesn't have to be an ending,” I said to her. “I don't want to walk away from you. I love you, Mom. I'm not angry. I just needed you to hear me. I just needed to finally have this conversation.”

“I'm glad you did,” she said, and a thousand pounds of weight lifted from my shoulders. I could have not imagined this going any better. It was worth the fear. “I can only promise that I'll be better.”

We ate our meal quietly, welcoming the violinist, trying to resume a sense of normalcy after a conversation that was certainly difficult for the both of us. We shared a bowl of limoncello gelato, and after lunch we walked around the souvenir shops. We relaxed, and talked about the house, and the tiny things – the plumbing, her plans for remodeling the basement, and what she was planning on making for dinner.

“You and Eli,” Mom said, and I was pleased that she remembered his name. “You aren't together anymore? Did something happen?”

I shifted my weight back and forth on my feet, lifting my shoulders, letting them fall.

"I'm not sure what we are right now," I confessed. "But I'm working on taking control of my life and going for what I want. I can tell you that much."

I spent the evening walking around by myself. Charlie told me he was tired and needed to take a nap back at the hotel before dinner, and while I wasn't hungry, I scoped out a few places – maybe we'd just grab pizza once more. Pizza and beer and a pay-per-view movie sounded like a nice way to end the trip. I didn't need to see any of the tourists traps – I had seen them all before, anyway.

I walked past the boutique shops, the interior lights glowing from chandeliers. The expensive dresses and hand-made jewelry; jade beads, pearls, golden chains, thin and frail as bone. I tried to wonder how it would feel, holding something so delicate in my hands. I tried to imagine myself wearing the gorgeous dress – pale pink silk – in the window – but all I could see was my own reflection, foggy in the glass, like I wasn't really standing there on the sidewalk.

I couldn't stop thinking of Eli. I really just wanted to get on a plane and go home. I wanted to crawl into my own bed, underneath the cheap, flannel sheets, and sleep a long, deep sleep. I missed the smell of my apartment – coffee, soy Country Apple candles, lavender Febreze.

I wanted to go home and find Eli. I wanted to fall into his arms and never come up for air.

Heart-aching, I called Charlie and left a voicemail to tell him I was heading back, and to be ready. We were getting pizza again. Pizza, beer, a movie. I wanted to get to bed early, because the sooner I was on that plane, the sooner I was home.

Still, I took the long route back. I stopped and watched some of the tourists take pictures with the knock-off Superheroes and Hello Kitties; their costumes minutely revised so that it wasn't quite copyright infringement. A missing piece on the belt, or bow on the ear. I watched a group of fluttery-eyed teenage girls take selfies in Times Square, squealing with delight, hugging each other. They clutched Starbucks in their hands instead of the local street-truck brew, thick and black and sipped out of dixie-sized paper cups. I never liked it.

I tried calling Charlie once more as I neared the hotel room, but it went straight to voicemail. I didn't care at this point – I would let him sleep if that's what he wanted. I was feeling so tired, heavy, my limbs like stone. I just wanted to sleep this feeling off.

But when I opened the door, and stepped inside into the dim room, glowing faintly with an unfamiliar flickering light, I noticed he wasn't there. At first, it was subtle – I couldn't hear him snoring, and he always snored.

As I walked into the room, however, I noticed the bed was made, and not just made, but untouched. He wasn't here, and his luggage wasn't here, and the bathroom light was shut off.

It took me a second to see him, standing by the window. When he turned, I saw a different face, and it wasn't Charlie's.

It was Eli. Eli, surrounded by countless candles, lit and dancing.

Eli, standing in front of me, the oversized window glowing an evening-blue from behind him, framing the city-scape, making him seem almost ethereal. This was unreal.

But it was all real. He was real. He was standing there, in front of me, and when I asked him where Charlie was, he told me that he'd left earlier. He caught an early flight back to LA. They had coordinated this – Charlie had called him, and told him where I was staying, and told him to come.

"Eli," I said softly. "I've missed you so much."

This was real. He wasn't a ghost. He was here, and he was smiling that same sardonic smile, and in awe I watched as he wordlessly knelt down in front of me, and extended in his hand a small, black box.

Inside, was a ring

This was real. This was happening. My heart, my heart, it both stopped and soared.

"I love you, Bailey," he whispered. "I read those pages you left. I read all of them. And I don't...I don't know how to do this, to live this life, without you. I need you with me. Can I try this again?"

I nodded, and through tears, he smiled.

"Will you marry me?"

A sob. A sigh. A single flight into his arms, where I clung to him, tears soaking into the pressed linen shirt he was wearing.

"Yes," I finally said. "I'll marry you."

CHAPTER 16
The Payoff

"What kind of wedding do you want?" Eli asked.

"Quick and cheap," I told him. "City Hall?"

We were laying outside, by the pool, drinking white wine and enjoying the balmy weather. It was the first time I had ever dared wear a bikini in front of anyone.

Eli rolled over, smiling sweetly.

"Maybe something a little bigger?" he asked. "Something with a theme."

"A theme, eh?" I smirked a little. "Fine. Here's a theme: *sleazy*. I'm wearing a red dress. You should wear something involving velvet. We'll have the ceremony and reception where we met, at the coffee shop. And you can invite all your porno friends. I'm fine with it. Charlie will be my Man of Honor, of course..."

I was actually getting into the idea. I could feel myself getting worked up, excited.

"Are you sure?" Eli asked. "About the crew, actors, you know. I mean, your mother will be in attendance, of course."

"I know," I laughed. "Won't that be a riot?"

So it was settled.

I bought the sluttiest red dress I could find. Eli wore a black-velvet suit. Charlie wore a dress like something straight out of Katy Perry's *Hot N' Cold* music video, at his insistence, and we married at the coffee shop. Our first kiss was across the counter, picture-perfect. Our wedding cake was another perfect replica of the one and only Dick Cake.

The total wedding budget: $5,000, including catering, buffet-style – steak, chicken, scallops, so many salads, and heaping plates of pasta marinara, pasta pesto, mushroom ravioli – because I was a pasta queen.

The look on my mother's face: *priceless*.

We danced to a soundtrack of early 2000's pop hits. We drank flutes of champagne under glittering lights, jam-packed into the makeshift dance floor in the middle of the cafe dining area. We partied hard.

But it's the vows I would remember. Mine were great, of course – but it was Eli's that took me by surprise.

Bailey, he'd said. *The truth is, I saw you in that coffee shop for over a month before you knocked that cup of coffee all over my new shirt. I used to wonder who you were, and what you liked, and whether you would ever be interested in a guy like me. I wanted to come up to you all those weeks, on my own, and talk to you. But the truth is, I was shy. I thought you were the most beautiful woman I had ever seen – and funny, too. So fucking funny, and smart, and charming. The truth is, Bailey, I wanted to marry you the day I met you. I thought about it on the drive home – I thought to myself, sitting in a soaking-wet T-shirt, I've gotta marry that woman someday. I have a find a way to get to know her. And I'm so glad that you spilled that cup of coffee on that fateful afternoon. I'm so glad you get to be my forever.*

I'm so glad you get to be my forever.

I know you're waiting for the payoff. So, here it is.

It was raining hard outside the hotel room. The lightening crashed from beyond the windows; the droplets like bullets against the glass.

The room, in a hotel overlooking the boats on Catalina Island, felt exotic – warm wooden floors, white linens, cream-colored walls. The bed was draped with an airy, gossamer fabric that I ran my fingers down nervously, my heart pounding, waiting in quiet prospect. My hair was dripping wet. My dress clung to my skin, to every curve, my breasts nearly exposed through the thin silk. I could still taste frosting on my lips.

Eli turned off the lights, and I lit the candles I had brought – jasmine, vanilla, sandalwood. I stood at the foot of the bed, facing him, and we looked at each other in a silent awe. We were drunk, in love, and finally joined together, in spirit, as one.

"My husband," I whispered, and he smiled.

"My wife."

He stepped towards me, taking my face in his hands, kissing me deeply. We fell like teenagers, wet and heated and full of hot blood, onto the bed. His fingers traced my jaw, down my neck, dragging slowly across my nape. I shivered, delicious, tasting the bourbon on his mouth and savoring the sound of his breaths, which were jagged and soft and something I had never heard before. His clothes were soaked; undoing the buttons was a fumbling game, which I took a great pleasure in. I wanted to undress him slowly. I wanted to see every glorious, shadowed, cut inch of him.

His shirt fell to the floor, and he got on his knees, undoing his pants above me. He had already kicked off his shoes, and I was still wearing my flats. Eli slid them off, one foot, kissing my ankle, then the other. I could see he was hard through the open fly of his slacks – I wanted so badly for him to slide out of his pants, to feel him back on top of me. I wanted to feel all of his weight, heavy and crushing. I craved him with an intensity that I previously never had words for – but this, this right now, was a fever, and I was bathed in musk and a consuming, feral desire.

I could hear the sound his belt, a gentle clang, as his pants hit the floor. He slid out of his boxers, until there he was, completely naked. I had seen him naked before, of course, but not like this – not like this. Not at all like this.

My heart gave a heavy pound. I could still feel the wet dress, clinging to my belly, my thighs, my heavy chest. I could see my nipples, hard and tender and wanting nothing but Eli's hands, peek through the fabric. I was practically undressed, but I had never in my life wanted so badly to be naked with someone.

"Take it off," I begged quietly. "Come here. I want you."

I was panting. Eli stood above me, a wolf in the darkness, darkly handsome and completely mine. I studied his mussed-up hair and full lips, and the way

they parted as if in pain as his eyes skimmed over me –
my bare feet, my exposed calves, thighs, to that slit still
covered in a thin, lace thong.

He knelt and slowly peeled the lace down my thighs,
down the long length of my legs, and tossed them aside.
He hitched my dress up above my waist, and as his
hands reached my hips I found myself unable to stop
myself from fondling my own breasts, my fingers
circling my nipples, so sensitive. I let it all flow, letting
every primal, animalistic urge free. I touched myself,
squeezed, feeling Eli's warm breath between my legs.

Eli kissed my feet, like I was sacred, and I was. I was
a goddess in this bed, and I felt the part. He kissed up
my legs, in-between my thighs, and when his mouth
reached that one, once untouched spot – that slit, my clit,
full and throbbing – I couldn't stop myself from arching
my back. I moaned softly. I buried my hands in his hair.

His tongue pressed against my clit, circling gently,
his lips sucking with an even greater skilled gentleness. I
could feel it seep into every cell in my body, like a
sepsis, like an infection that I wanted no cure for. I
wanted this fever to last forever. I wanted to feel him
between my legs, worshipping me with his mouth, with
the sounds of the whipping rain outside, pelting the
windows, forever.

I wanted him, and only him, forever.

He kissed me once more there, lifting his head, and
our eyes met. As he stood, I could see his hard cock –
long, thick, standing straight. He stroked it, toying with
himself in front of me, teasing.

"How would you feel if I came like this?" he asked, devilish. "How would you feel if I came, just touching myself to you? Would you like that?"

I sat up, grabbed him, kissed him intensely. I bit his bottom lip with my teeth, tasting a faint metallic.

"I'll kill you," I breathed, and we laughed. "I need you to fuck me."

Eli responded immediately: he pushed me lightly, back down onto the bed, and I fell with my hair like ribbons behind me. He fingered the straps of my dress, lowering them from my shoulders slowly, pulling my dress down at the hem. First, my shoulders were exposed, then my breasts, the curves of my stomach, my waist, my hips, my legs.

When the dress hit the floor, I was completely naked, save for the subtle moonlight that kissed us both so tenderly.

He ran his tongue in small circles around my nipples, sucking softly. It felt so fucking incredible; an extension of that craving spot between my legs. He stayed there for a minute, one breast in his hand, the other in his mouth, taking turns, savoring my body with his fingers and lips and tongue.

He took a deep breath, taking me all in. The smell of my skin, the sweat, candles mingling in the air.

"You are so beautiful," he said, and the awe in his voice was real. His voice was thick, heavy with lust. "I can't believe you're mine."

He leaned forward, his weight pressing atop me. His arms reached around to hold me, to stroke my face and hair, and for awhile we kissed. Our mouths melded, formed together, our tongues weaving gently, tenderly, fiercely, full-blooded. We tasted each other, savored each breath, breathed into each other, breathed for each other. Our hearts beat against one another, our skin pressed together. The bed felt as if it had caught fire.

"I'm ready," I whispered into his ear. "I need you."

He met my gaze with a sweetly taut intensity, drunk on this moment, his body rigid with yearning. I could feel every muscle.

He reached down, between his legs, and I could feel his tip against my opening – barely there, barely touching.

He teased me, at first. He pressed the head against me, moving it around, watching me writhe in response. He seemed to take a certain delight in the way my back arched, or the way my toes curled, or the way I begged so softly. I said his name, over and over again: *Eli, Eli.*

In one sharp thrust, he was fully inside me. I gasped, feeling the sharpness, at first harsh – unexpected despite being so desperately craved. There was the rush of pain, rising up my thighs, into my belly, that slowly gave way into something deeper, something greater. A feeling of pleasure, as he began to move so slowly, like a serpent in the water.

My hands found his back, my nails clawing gently. I found myself clinging to him, moaning against his ear, begging for him to go deeper, wanting nothing but to keep drowning in the depths of measurable ache and bliss. There was so much pleasure in the pain, too. I wanted the waves to continue. I wanted to ride this current for as long as I could.

I could feel every inch of him inside me, his skin hot against mine, our bodies finally one, our mouths pressed together deeply, kissing, lips parting, eyes locked onto one another, studying each other. I learned the curve of his mouth, his shoulders, the way his hair smelled when wet with rain. I learned the way his sweat tasted, and he learned the way my body moved along with his. He could taste my skin, my own sweat, and breathe in every dancing pheromone.

Something was building up inside of me. I could feel it my belly, between my legs, across every inch of my skin. I didn't think this would be possible – not now, not the first time, and I was okay with that. But here I was, feeling it, feeling it build, feeling the mounting pleasure like a flower blooming – slowly, each petal unfolding one-by-one.

I came, moaning his name, my mouth in his hair, his face buried into my shoulder. We clung to each other, desperate, soaked in one another, and he whispered that he was so close.

"I'm..." he started, giving one final, hard thrust. "Oh, God..."

I could feel his cum, hot, shooting inside of me. I could feel it flow between my legs, seeping out softly, smelling of warmth, of saltwater.

He didn't pull out right away – I didn't want him to. I wanted to hold onto this moment for as long as possible. I wanted to memorize his face. I needed to memorize his drowsy smile, and the sound of his fading breath, and the way he looked at me with such a passionate love.

I couldn't believe that I was laying beneath him. Our bodies were still joined. We were still one.

The rain outside still rang like bullets. I could hear the crackling of the wooden candle wicks, and see the subtle golden glow dance above us. I could see my husband, my Eli, laying above me, studying me, too.

"I love you," he whispered. "Bailey Finch."

We lay next to each other, listening to the rain, letting it all seep in. Not letting the moment slip away. I would hold onto this, to this night, tucking it away like the tiniest note: each moan and gasp and subtle move scribbled in black ink, documented.

Except instead of ink, I had the dress on the floor. I had the beautiful ache between my legs. I had the mark on my shoulder where Eli had bitten down, or on his bottom lip where I had bitten down, still tender and red.

I took a thousand photographs, storing them away in my mind, and laying in my husband's arms, fell asleep and dreamt of them.

He woke me in the morning: coffee and handcuffs, of all things. I was sore, too sore for a round two, perhaps – but Eli had something else in mind.

The handcuffs were fuzzy, soft, unthreatening. He kissed my cheek, my jaw, my nose, playful.

Obediently, still warm and heavy with sleep, I lifted

my hands above my head, and felt him clasp my wrists.
I spread myself out, all for him, still completely naked.
He wore his boxers, his hair a delightful mess from the
night before.

Outside, the sun spilled golden through the window.
We were both rinsed anew in morning light.

He kissed my legs again, taking his sweet time
teasing. He kissed and pressed and swirled his tongue,
his breath hot against my slit, my clit swollen and my
toes curling with every caress. His fingernails gently
scraped down my thighs, sending a shiver up my spine.
He kept going, slowly, so slowly, until I could feel the
inevitable rise. My breath hitched; my wrists happily
struggled against the soft handcuffs.

I came against his mouth, quickly – quicker than I
wanted to. I moaned softly, feeling the sensation move
through my body like a slow, dreamy drug.

Eli stood, touched a finger to his lips, grinning.

"Good morning," he said. "My beautiful wife."

I blinked into the sunlight, with Eli slowly coming
into view. I was still in the warm haze of post-orgasm. I
hadn't come down yet. I didn't want to.

"Hi," I breathed, dreamily. "My incredible husband."

We spent the rest of our honeymoon sailing on the
water, the saltwater mist tangling our hair, the crystalline
deep broadcasting to us the many creatures, the coral,
the dancing life below. I fell asleep on the white, hot
sand, topless, drunk on Bahama Mamas and the smell of
sunscreen. Drunk on Eli, effortlessly cool in his Ray
Bans, lounging in swim trunks, soaked from a dive, his

skin glistening.

I could do this forever, I thought. If I had to, I wouldn't change a thing. I had never been more thankful for the train-wreck that led me here, to this man.

To the story of us.

I never imagined myself walking a red carpet. But the truth is, I never imagined myself in a multitude of situations. I never imagined myself working for a time at a chic magazine, or writing a hit piece, or even a hit novel. A novel that ended up being a runaway bestseller, of all things, to my completely sincere shock. And I never imagined falling in love with a former porn star, who would fall in love with me, too. Happily ever after, as the stories say.

I never imagined myself smiling against the flashing lights of a hundred cameras, answering questions on the gown I was wearing – who designed it, who styled my hair, who did my makeup – my response being only a wink. I'm not sure you'd ask those kinds of questions to the men here, would you?

I never imagined myself sitting in a theater, surrounded by celebrities, watching my husband on the silver-screen, in awe, feeling such pride. Eli had made it, he was here, he had done it. Even from a mathematical standpoint, even despite his dalliance in the Adult Industry, there existed still a mountain of outstanding odds that he had conquered.

And I never imagined...

Standing barefoot, in the doorway of our New York apartment, wearing one of Eli's button-downs. My hair, messy from sex, and my face still flushed.

I slipped a box from underneath the pillow. A watch box, wrapped in plain paper and tied with a red bow.

Eli, curiously taking the box from me, studying it intently.

"Are you trying to tell me what time is?" he asked. "I already own a watch."

He was still laying in bed, rolled over onto his back. His fingers worked carefully, untying the bow, carefully folding back the paper.

The test fell with a soft thud onto the bedspread. Eli looked at it, awestruck, and then – as I never could have imagined, there was a tearful smile. He held the note I had written in his hands – *it's time to get ready for our next chapter!*

"I'm gonna be a daddy," he said. "I can't believe it. You're pregnant. Bailey!"

He jumped up, hugging me tightly. We kissed a thousand times, and he kissed my belly, and he held my face in his hands.

"I love you, I love you, I love you."

A couple weeks later, I had an ultrasound. I framed the photo and placed it in my office, next to a stack of my freshly-printed novels, awaiting signature. They'd be sent out to a few select readers later that week.

As I set the photo down, I looked at the cover. My fingers skimmed the soft, almost creamy paper. I could have never imagined this.

RATED-XXX, the cover said. *A Virgin. A Porn Star. A Comedy.*

Soon we would be a family of three. Soon there

would be a thousand more chapters. And we, together, would stumble forward joyfully, fuck-ups and all, into our happily ever after.

That thought alone was sweeter than any slice of cake.

END SCENE.

Mya Oh is an author, mother, and amateur baker. *HOT WET TRAINWRECK* is her debut novel.

When not writing, she enjoys spending time exploring the woods of her rural town. She currently resides on the East Coast with her husband, two sons, and ginger tabby cat.

For any inquiries, or to connect:

Email:
oh.mya.books@gmail.com

Twitter:
@Oh_Mya_Books

Instagram:
@oh.mya.author